I0682376

THE GOOD GRIFFIN

THAT OLD BLACK MAGIC: HEART'S DESIRED MATE

J. C. McKENZIE

This is a work of fiction. Names, characters, places, and incidents
are either the product of the author's imagination or are used
fictiously, and any resemblance to actual persons living or dead,
business establishments, events, or locales, is entirely coincidental.

The Good Griffin

COPYRIGHT © 2018 by J. C. McKenzie

All rights reserved. No part of this book may be used or
reproduced in any manner whatsoever without written permission
of the author except in the case of brief quotations embodied in
critical articles or reviews.

Contact Information: jcmckenzie@jcmckenzie.ca

Cover Art by Monica La Porta

Publishing History:
JCM Publications First Edition, 2018

ISBN-13: 978-1-7752251-5-7 (digital)
ISBN-13: 978-1-7752251-4-0 (print)

To Melissa Snark.

CONTENTS

The Heart's Desire Spell

"Pray, hear my words, Ceridwen,
Mother of Magic,
Goddess who is Wise.
Upon this full moon dark, this season of ice,
When the mists between the worlds are thin,
I call upon your power to arise and come to me.
Heart's desire called forth.
Ceridwen, assess my worth.
Freedom from slavery, naked in your rites.
Liberated from fear and doubt this night.
Before the dawn, deliver my heart's delight and desire.
Love is the law unto all beings.
My will be done, so mote it be."

In Melissa Snark's *Love is the Law*, Damian is a ruthless villain intent on a witch's downfall.

Every good story, though, has two sides.

This is Damian's...

CHAPTER ONE

A SOUND HAMMERING

Monday morning, November 5th

Cool air rushed past Lucy as she stood precariously on the top rung of a step ladder. She clenched her teeth and swung the hammer.

Bam. Bam. Bam.

The strong aroma of coffee wafted from inside the coffee shop, along with the welcoming din of customers. The espresso machine whooshed and sprayed, the grinder ground fresh beans, and her employee, Tanner, called out completed orders. The Rise & Grind. Her coffee shop.

Hers.

The morning rush had started and at the rate she was going, she wouldn't have the window boarded up until lunch. Not that she was inept, but every customer stopped on the street to greet her and ask how she was coping. Though she valued her customers and appreciated their concern, the constant interruptions meant she hadn't nailed more than a single board in place, much less made anything secure.

What happened? Who did this? Do you need any help?

Her responses to the constant barrage of questions sounded hollow, even to her. The anger boiling in her veins from the broken window had dissipated, leaving her drained and as cold as the winter's day.

Why would someone throw a brick through her window?

Teenagers on a dare? A dissatisfied customer? Coffee hater? None of these possibilities fit with the people of Stillwater, California, a small town nestled in the Sierra Nevada Mountains.

She needed to finish up and help Tanner before he got really swamped. She wiped her hands on her black jeans before bracing against the rough board again.

"It's a little crooked," a deep voice said from behind her.

"Wha—" She partially turned.

Whack!

Mid-swing the hammer slammed into her thumb holding the nail. Pain shot up from her hand. Lucy winced and pulled her arm in. Her thumb screamed. With a deep breath, she turned perilously on the ladder to face Detective Damian Charming.

Despite his name and appearance, there was really nothing charming about him.

She shook her hand by her side, hiding the action from Damian with her body. She wanted to suck on her thumb, or cry, "Ow, ow, ow," but not with Damian a foot away.

Handsome, in a glass-cutting way, Damian peered up at her. His arrogant full lips smirking and his intense golden gaze laughing. Dressed in dark jeans and a fitted sweater to stave off the cold, he radiated confidence and power. Of course, the warm clothing was for show. He probably didn't need any of it.

Meeeeeow, her inner lynx chose now to pipe up.

Not now, Whispurr.

When Lucy first met him, Damian had been swoon worthy in uniform, and then he had to go get promoted. Now, dressed in "civilian clothes," he was beyond devastating to look at. With straight black hair curling slightly behind his ears to his jawline, tan, almost golden skin, and a tall powerful build, his presence evoked all sorts of naughty fantasies.

Until she remembered she hated him.

Or he opened his mouth.

Or both.

"Are you okay?" Damian narrowed his eyes and leaned to the side, probably trying to get a better look at her hidden hand.

To anyone else he might sound sincere, concerned even, but Lucy wasn't fooled. Damian Charming was a self-absorbed elitist. She was probably one of the few who knew his true identity as a griffin—the half eagle, half lion, lord of all beasts.

"Lucy?" Damian frowned.

He expected an answer. What had he asked again? Was she okay? Not in the slightest.

"Fine, thank you." She climbed down the ladder with as much dignity as she could muster. She'd pounded in enough nails to hold the board in place until she had more time to deal with the disaster of her café's storefront.

She glanced at her work. Dammit, Damian was right. It was crooked.

"Hi, Lucy." Damian's partner stepped around the bulk of Damian to smile at her.

"Hi, Mateo. How've you been?"

"Pretty good. Sorry to hear about the window." Hispanic with dark hair and dark eyes, Detective Mateo Savage was serious and quiet. Too reserved for her taste, but Lucy always had a soft spot for the panther shifter. Maybe because they were both felines. Or maybe because he was a stand-up guy and always respectful and courteous.

Honestly, the detectives should swap surnames for the sake

3

of accuracy.

"Yeah," she said, addressing his window comment. "Not the way I wanted to start my Monday." She folded the ladder. "Have you heard from Jewel recently?"

"Of course. My sister couldn't escape me if she tried." Mateo winked. His younger sister left the den in the fall to attend college and the protective detective was having a hard time with it, no matter what he tried to tell anyone else. "Let's go inside and get your statement."

"Sounds good." She glanced at Damian.

He glowered.

She stumbled. The ladder slipped from her grip, but she caught it before it fell to the snow-dusted sidewalk. She readjusted her hold. "Isn't investigating random acts of vandalism a little beneath you two?"

Damian and Mateo exchanged a look.

"Things are slow," Damian bit out.

Geez. How was the lack of crime her fault? She could up it, of course, but he wouldn't be around to solve his own murder.

Mateo frowned at Damian before turning to her. "Here, Luce. Let me take the ladder for you. Damian will get us coffees and we can take your statement."

Before she could argue, Mateo extracted the ladder from her clutches, and Damian held the door open, his rings glinting in the morning light. One of those silver rings shielded his essence from nosy supernaturals and perpetuated his warlock image. Lucy didn't know why. She'd never met a griffin before, but Damian didn't strike her as the type to balk from unwanted attention. He had to be hiding his nature out of necessity.

Lucy shivered. What on earth would be powerful enough to take down someone as formidable as Damian?

"Thanks," she said to both men, and walked past them into the café.

Warm heavenly-scented air from her coffee shop rushed

out—strong and potent. She let the moment wash over her. Muted outside, the cacophony of customers chatting, dishes clanking and the espresso machine steaming milk greeted her unhindered and at full volume.

Tanner, her barista and the only other full-time employee at Rise & Grind, glanced up from behind the counter. Panic splayed across his face.

"I have to help Tanner first."

"You want us to wait?" Damian grumbled.

Lucy bit her tongue. Did he not see how busy it was? This business put food on the table and a roof over her head. She wouldn't let it languish and risk dissatisfied customers or burnt out staff to appease the mighty lord griffin.

Why, yes. She wanted them to wait. She'd chew him out, but he really didn't get it. And his lack of interpersonal skills hadn't stopped him from helping her in a prickly situation a few years ago. Damian Charming, for all his faults, had come to her rescue. And bonus points to him, even though he'd seen her at her weakest, he hadn't thrown it in her face.

Yeah, she hated him...but sometimes she felt something else entirely when she saw him. Something just as strong and infuriating, and too disturbing to name.

She turned to walk away.

Damian grunted.

The din of the busy café muffled Mateo's words. "Dude. Ease up."

"Look at the line. We're slammed," Lucy said over her shoulder. "Can my statement *please* wait?"

"Well, you already disturbed any evidence the perpetrator would've left, so I guess waiting won't do any more harm."

Ugh. All the tenderness for the cop fled. Without a backward glance, she walked away and slipped behind the counter. She pulled off her oversized knit sweater, leaving a simple T-shirt, and tied a serving apron around her waist.

"About time!" Tanner's harried expression was almost comical.

"Sorry. That took longer than I thought."

"The window or the police?"

"Both, actually."

"Is it done?"

She shook her head. "Not even close."

"Balls." Tanner squeezed her shoulder. He called out an order and slid a to-go cup across the countertop.

The line moved quickly with Lucy at the helm and Tanner diligently completing the orders. They worked well together. The partially boarded window blocked the usual sunlight from streaming in, but the café's internal lighting provided a soft glow.

After a few minutes and several customers, Damian stood in front of the counter, gaze forward, lost in thought. He always got the coffees when he came in with Mateo. He was such a control freak, he didn't trust his own partner to get the order right even though it was the same every time.

"Damian?" Lucy rose an eyebrow.

"Huh?"

"The usual for you two?"

"Yeah." He pulled out his wallet and rifled through the bills. "I didn't mean to give you a hard time earlier."

"About the crooked board or disturbing the evidence?" She plucked the bills from his outstretched hand.

"Both." His lips remained pressed firmly in a thin line, losing the fullness she sometimes found herself dreaming about.

She collected the change from the cash register and held it out for him.

He shook his head.

"Thanks." She dumped the coins into the tip jar and returned his stare. "Tanner will get your drinks."

Lightning flashed in Damian's gaze.

After an embarrassing encounter during a run, she'd discovered not only his nature, but his derision toward her and her abilities. He told her the idea of her confronting her father about his attempts to extort and then kidnap her was absurd and she should leave the fighting to the big boys—in other words, him. Sure, he had a point, but his words and the way he spoke them gave away more than the simple truth. They said what he really thought of her.

Nothing ruined a fantasy faster than discovering her crush viewed her as inept when she stood naked in front of him in a moonlit forest. That night could've played out in so many other ways. More pleasurable ways. But, on par with the rest of her life, reality paled in comparison to her fantasies.

Lucy leaned to the side and called out, "Next?"

Damian grunted and moved out of the way.

Heat pressed against Lucy's face as she steamed the milk and finished the last of the orders from the morning rush.

"I'm sure your Monday will improve." An attractive businessman with silver hair smiled. His even white teeth invited her to scrub the scowl from her face.

"Pardon?" She slid his latté across the counter.

The man jerked his head toward the window. "Heard some of the other customers talking about it. Bad luck."

She blew a stray strand of light brown hair from her face. Bad luck was her middle name. She'd deal with this like she dealt with all the other bumps in the road—a ruthless, systematic approach to solving the problem, followed by shredding apart a hapless rabbit in the neighboring forest. Maybe two. Filling her belly with food she caught herself always put a little pep in her step.

"Does this sort of thing happen often?" he asked.

Her stomach sank. "It didn't used to."

First, Mrs. Bee's flower shop, now her store. Could the incidents be related? In a small town like Stillwater, the likelihood of two vandals was low to non-existent.

The man frowned, accentuating his chiseled features. "Shame. I was thinking of investing in the area. I might have to re-evaluate."

Lucy studied the man in front of her. He didn't appear or smell supernatural, but he exuded confidence. He wore a thick silver ring around his index finger. A charm maybe? To hide his true nature from everyone else? Stillwater rarely got non-supernatural visitors, and when they did, the strong aversion spells generally made their stay short.

The man looked at her expectantly, but she had no clue what to say besides to thank him for his business and wish him a pleasant stay in Stillwater. After he left, she grabbed a coffee—Americano soy misto—and made her way to the detectives.

Mateo sprawled in one of the lounge chairs. His cup sat on the table beside Damian's, but the seat across from him remained empty. Instead, Damian's sweater lay strewn across the cushion.

"Where's Damian?" She pulled up a chair.

Mateo smiled and straightened. He slid his phone into his pocket. "Righting a wrong?"

She almost snorted. If he was out committing random acts of kindness, he wouldn't make it back before the lunch rush.

Mateo's expression gave nothing away, but his shirt told another story.

"Why is your shirt wet?"

Mateo scowled. "Incident with a faulty tap."

Lucy glanced at the kitchen doors where her friend Keira had been washing dishes. The bear shifter wasn't an employee, but she'd rushed over to help when she spotted the shattered window.

"A faulty tap?"

"Yup."

Well, okay then. She didn't believe a word, but if he didn't want to talk about it, she wasn't going to pry. She relaxed into her chair. "Can you take my statement?"

"Sure thing, Luce."

The door opened and cool air flowed in with Damian. He clutched a hammer in one hand and her ladder in the other. His shirt stretched across his strong chest.

Her mouth dropped open.

Damian strode across the room toward the counter, seemingly unaware of the appreciative glances cast his way by a number of the female patrons, and returned the ladder to Tanner. When had the detective grabbed it? How did she not notice? How had she missed the hammering?

Oh, god. Hammering. She squeezed her eyes shut at the dirty thought. Why did she have to think of that now?

Why'd he have to look so good in a simple T-shirt?

"Did you finish boarding the window?" she asked when he walked over. Out of all the questions rampaging through her brain, she was glad she settled on that one.

"Well, someone had to fix it." He flopped down in his chair. His lips curled up in a smug smile.

Lucy clutched the handle of her mug.

Take a deep breath, Whispurr said.

He can't help being arrogant. He's a griffin, lord of all beasts.

Take another breath. The first one didn't work, Whispurr prodded.

"Thank you for *fixing* the board." She was doing just fine patching up her place without him, thank you very much.

Take another breath, psycho, Whispurr said. *He's being nice.*

Her irritation slowly flowed from her veins and dissipated. Her lynx had a point. Damian went out of his way to help her. Again.

"I wish you'd have waited until we arrived before cleaning up," Damian said.

Quick! Breathe.

Was he trying to piss her off? "I couldn't close down for the day and lose business because some punk decided to take out their angst on my window. Monday morning is one of our busiest times. I also couldn't have customers walking through glass or sitting by a gaping hole in the window in November with a brick as their centerpiece."

Damian opened his mouth to speak.

She thunked her mug on the table between then and kept going. "I arrived at work an hour before opening and called it in. I called my insurance company next and took pictures of the scene before I touched a thing. These are the directions the police station gave me when I called, so giving me crap about following orders, after the fact, doesn't accomplish anything except making my day worse than it already is."

Mateo's dark brows rose.

Damian's intense gaze softened. He leaned back. His shoulders relaxed into the chair and the fabric of his shirt stretched even more across his chest. "I wasn't trying to give you crap, Luce."

"Seems like it to me," she grumbled and crossed her arms. Oh god. Did he have to call her Luce? Her nickname spoken with his deep rumbling voice was more than she could handle right now.

Mateo coughed.

She glanced over.

He took a deep sip from his coffee mug and avoided eye contact.

"Did you catch a scent?" Damian shifted in his seat and

glared at his partner.

Wow. If looks could kill...

She shook her head. "Nothing out of the ordinary. This is a busy place with the club, daycare and courthouse. The area is filled with too many scent signatures. Besides, I rely more on sight and hearing for hunting." Despite the low crime rate, the detectives wouldn't take this case. Too small. They'd most likely pass it off to some junior officers.

Damian's head snapped up from his coffee. "You're not going after this person on your own, are you?"

"Of course not." Lucy huffed. She needed more information first. Maybe she should call Laura. In addition to running the Clover Club, the town's upscale bar, her friend had a side business working as a private investigator. Or maybe she'd ask Kiera for help. Bears had an excellent sense of smell.

"What else can you tell us about the vandalism?" Damian asked, gaze hardening. He removed a notepad from his pocket, but his attention remained focused on her.

Heat bloomed in her chest. His gaze unsettled her. He probably didn't need to write anything down. His expression told her he'd commit every word, gesture, blink and facial tic to memory. He'd given her the same look when she'd crumbled and told him about her father.

Her heart hammered against her breastbone, but she forced another deep breath in and out before her lynx hissed at her. Lucy grabbed her mug and took a deep sip. The creamy coffee coated her mouth and warmed her belly.

He was a detective for a reason. He'd mercilessly track down the vandal. If Mateo wasn't his partner, she'd worry about the griffin skipping the justice system altogether and exacting his own punishment on the criminal.

"There's not much to tell," she said. "I got to work and found the front window broken. Nothing appears to have been taken and it didn't look like the person entered the café."

Damian nodded. "What time did you arrive to work?"

"Around six."

His eyebrows rose. "The call came in at 0630."

"I needed to calm down first and make a plan."

He scribbled something down without looking. "Any note?"

"No. No note. No suspicious strangers loitering nearby. No threats beforehand. No social media videos claiming responsibility either."

"Cute." His gaze pinned her in the seat. Did he study his lovers with this much intensity?

Heat crept up her neck and flooded her face. Images of Damian watching her while trapping her with his naked body flashed through her mind.

No!

She couldn't fantasize about a man who clearly dismissed her.

Damian's scribbling faltered. His nose flared and his gaze broke away.

Oh no. Please don't let griffins read minds. As a shifter, she could catch elevated heart rates and certain scents associated with intense emotions. She never stopped to consider a griffin would have the same capabilities.

A different kind of heat spread to replace the desire. If only she could melt away in her seat. Mateo probably picked up on the scent, too. Her muscles itched to glance his way and check, but she resisted the urge. Maybe she should bolt from her seat and run away.

Whispurr coughed. *Because that wouldn't add to the embarrassment.*

Why did this pesky attraction to the griffin keep flaring up this way? He insulted her. He was condescending and a jerk. Dismissive. She hated him. Right?

Right?

Apparently, her own brain housed a field of chirping crickets. Perfect.

Mateo chuckled into his coffee cup.

Lucy turned to stare him down at the same time as Damian.

Mateo shook his head. "Sorry. Funny cat meme." He waved his phone at them, screen turned away before stuffing it in his pocket. The corner of his eyes crinkled.

Damian cleared his throat. "Did you have any late night customers? Did anyone loiter a little longer this morning or seem unusually interested in the vandalism?"

"No, no and of course, yes. This is a small town and a smashed window is the most exciting thing to happen since Laura and a tiger shifter chased the same fugitive down the middle of Main Street during a parade. Everyone wants to know about the vandalism."

Damian grunted. "Any new customers?"

Her shoulders sagged. "I always get a few new customers—people passing through or in town for court. As you know, the non-supernatural rarely stick around long."

"You said you took pictures."

She nodded.

"Can you text them to me?"

She hesitated.

He prattled off his number. And waited.

"What, now?" she asked.

"Please." His gaze bore into hers.

She pulled her phone from her front pocket, pulled up the photos and glanced again at Damian. His focus remained intent on her, gaze blazing like a fire pit.

"All of them?"

"Yes."

She swiped, tapped and entered the phone number she already committed to memory. Heat suffused her face. Maybe she should've asked for his number again so she didn't look like such a stalker. She memorized it from the last time she used it. Who even remembered phone numbers these day? Lucy May, that's who.

Damian's phone vibrated. He glanced at the screen before turning back to her. He pressed on. "What time did you leave work last night?"

"Around ten."

His pen stopped. "You close at seven on Sundays."

Why did her traitorous heart skip at the knowledge he knew her hours? Everyone within a twenty-mile radius with a caffeine addiction knew her hours.

"I was prepping."

His dark browns dug farther in. "Do you always stay so late?"

"You need this for the investigation?"

"It establishes routine," Damian said. "Whether it played a part in the criminal's actions, we'll find out later. As a side note, though. You work ridiculous hours."

"Well I'm *a ridiculous* person."

He pressed his lips into a flat line.

"I make a living selling coffee. I also run on the stuff."

He shook his head and flipped his notebook closed. "Those hours aren't healthy, Luce. Eventually, something is going to give."

"You say that like you care." She spat out the words, but she knew the truth. Despite all his arrogance, he cared enough to shield her from harm. Damian might've glimpsed her weakness—desperately wanting to belong—but in the process, he'd given himself away. Damian had a savior complex, specifically with women. With her.

Mateo shifted in his seat. When she glanced over, he'd found a shiny floor tile that fascinated him.

Damian stiffened. "Maybe I do."

CHAPTER TWO

A CONSPIRACY OF RAVENS

Damian wanted to reach across the pedestal table and shake some sense into Lucy. He didn't trust himself, though. The moment his hands touched that dainty soft skin of hers, he'd move to explore her body. And if he knew anything about the feisty lynx shifter sitting across from him spitting fire from her eyes, it was that she had no time for him. His advances would be unwelcome

"You care?" Lucy sounded incredulous. Her eyebrows shot up to her hairline. She straightened in her seat. Petite and lean, she embodied her feline nature. Tawny hair cascaded around her heart-shaped face and brought out the honey-hazel of her almond-shaped eyes. Her Cupid's bow lips pouted naturally and her dark brows furrowed when she concentrated. He wanted to claim every inch of her body.

His partner tried his best to blend in with the chair, unsuccessfully. Nice backup. He could use some intervention.

Maybe I do? Why the hell had he said that? Lucy made it perfectly clear she had zero interest in him. Now she gaped at him like he spontaneously sprouted five heads.

You need to take her, Hippo growled. His griffin had nagged him to pursue Lucy non-stop since he met the lynx shifter, not understanding the complexities of human courtship. To Hippo, it was simple. Damian wanted Lucy, so Damian should take her. It never crossed the featherhead's mind that she might be unwilling. Why would anyone not want a griffin?

Damian knew better. And he certainly would never take anything not freely given.

The door chimed as more customers poured in from the cold.

Lucy continued to stare at him and wait for a response.

He cleared his throat. Again. "Of course, I care. If you crash and burn, where am I going to get a decent cup of coffee in this town?"

Hippo groaned.

Mateo rolled his eyes at the ceiling.

Damian winced.

"I'll try not to inconvenience you." Lucy stood up and turned to his partner. Her hazel gaze sparkled with intensity, like citrine or the brighter part of a tiger's eye. "Thank you for coming. If there's no more questions, I need to get back to work."

Mateo nodded and stood to shake her hand. "We'll need you to sign the statement once we've typed it up."

"Sure thing." She walked away without a glance at Damian or a goodbye. The entire time she spoke with Mateo, Damian remained sitting. She left a wake of her scent—mischief and mayhem wrapped around him in a whisper of a caress. He drew in a deep breath, savoring the petal soft fragrance.

Mateo turned to him.

"Don't say it."

"Real smooth."

His fist twitched. No, he couldn't punch his partner for

making a painfully accurate observation. He found it hard to find any fault in Mateo, which was probably why the panther shifter was one of his only friends in town.

After his parents and brother were murdered in Miami, Mateo had hauled his little sister to Stillwater so fast the guns hadn't finished smoking. This sleepy town became a safe place for Mateo to raise and protect Jewel, his scared ten-year-old sister. She'd grown up, thanks to papa Mateo, and left to attend Eastern Oregon University this fall. Strong and focused from working in the military and then construction, his partner could hold his own in almost any situation, but not being able to protect his sister from the big bad real world at a distance proved to be Mateo's downfall. He'd been on edge for weeks.

"You're a great cop," Mateo said. "Why are you such an idiot with her?"

Damian glanced over to the counter where Lucy had taken up position. He didn't need to worry. She wasn't paying either of them any attention.

"I don't know," he said. Damn she was hot when she was angry.

His blood had boiled since he got the call this morning. How dare someone attack Lucy? His griffin energy coiled around him. Jealous, covetous and potent. It had done that a lot lately, at least whenever Lucy was involved. He'd have to go for a run. In the meantime, he pushed the pressure down. He'd find who tried to harm her. He turned back to his partner.

Mateo shook his head.

"What?"

"Man, you have it bad."

"Shut up." Bad enough the whole precinct knew about his infatuation—hard to dupe investigators—but his partner teased him about it mercilessly.

Mateo grunted and reached down to grab Damian's sweater. "Come on. I assume we're taking this case. We should start canvassing."

Damian snatched his sweater from his partner and pulled it on. He didn't need it. His griffin nature provided enough heat for him to stalk naked through the streets on this winter day, but he had no interest in announcing his abilities. Let the town think he was a warlock who wore charmed rings. Let them underestimate his strength and power.

Too bad his abilities couldn't shield him from making an ass of himself. "Just give me a second, there's something I need to do first."

"Fine." Mateo settled back in his chair and pulled his phone out.

Damian studied his partner as he pulled up a game app. He'd assumed Mateo's uncharacteristically brusque behavior was a side effect of his empty-nest syndrome. Was something else bothering him? He hesitated. Should he say something?

Not now.

He left his partner to glare at his phone and stalked toward the counter. He needed to talk to Lucy.

Finally, Hippo perked up.

Not that kind of talk.

Ugh. Hippo flopped back down.

He was in love with the lynx shifter. Painfully so. Sometime between her serving him the first latté with some serious snark and her asking for his help with a personal situation, he'd fallen for her, hard. But she wasn't for him. Not only was she not a griffin—good luck finding one of those—but he was ninety-nine percent sure she hated his guts. At least until today.

His mind drifted to the night he inadvertently interrupted her run by snagging the hare she'd chased. Not knowing the sleek lynx who bounded into the clearing was a shifter, his considerable appetite turned to the newcomer.

Lucy had quickly shifted and he realized he'd almost

attacked the woman he'd spent months admiring at the coffee shop. He could've left without revealing his identity, but something took over his common sense that night and within minutes, he stood in front of Lucy. Naked.

Back in the present, Lucy mumbled something to Tanner and slipped from behind the counter to head toward her office. Damian altered his course and followed. Lucy's petite body moved with efficient determination, yet remained soft and graceful. Just like her lynx form. Beautiful and lethal, she could handle herself, but the need to surge ahead and protect her made his skin itch. It took every ounce of control not to bellow at everyone to move out of his way or simply throw them from his path. Deep breaths, Damian told himself. *Behave.*

"Lucy," he hissed when he got near.

She kept walking, her footsteps light and almost indiscernible with the constant babble of surrounding customers.

He reached forward and clamped a hand on her shoulder. His fingers gripping the soft fabric of her T-shirt.

Lucy jumped.

"We need to talk," Damian growled in her ear. He steered her to the office and shut the door behind them.

On the soft click of the door, she spun around, her honey gaze flashing under the fluorescent lights of her office. "You could've asked to speak with me. No need to manhandle."

"Maybe I like manhandling you?" he said. He'd picked up on her arousal earlier. What dirty thoughts flew through that beautiful head of hers? He leaned forward, all his senses on high alert. Her heart raced, pounding so hard an ordinary human would hear it, and her gaze remained trained on him. Could Lucy finally be warming up to him?

"Surprising. Figured you'd like to keep your claws clean instead of soiling them with a lowdown Lynx."

Okay, maybe she wasn't warming up to him, yet. Maybe

she'd been thinking of something else.

Someone else.

Hippo bristled and clawed at his brain.

Instantaneous rage boiled in his blood. He glanced around the office space. If only he could grab the padded chair and hurl it across the small room. Who the hell would she be thinking about?

Hippo screeched. *Track down the asshole. We'll tear his eyes out.*

"Well?" Lucy folded her arms.

Well what? Damian took a deep breath and let the red haze fade from his vision. He had no idea what she meant with the lowdown lynx comment and he couldn't stop her from thinking about other men, but he could protect her. He needed to continue on as planned. "Could this be related to your father?"

Lucy froze. "You think he's back?"

"Doesn't really fit his money-leaching extortion-attempting ways, but I'm not ruling it out."

She rubbed her bare arms.

"Any contact?" If that vile creature had tried to weasel his way back into Lucy's life, promises or no promises, he'd rend the man's limbs from his body.

"None."

He nodded. No contact didn't mean Lucy's father wasn't involved. "If you hear anything or see him..."

"I'll let you know."

Damian hesitated. "You don't need to worry, Luce."

He had her back. He'd protect her. Hell, a minute ago, he was ready to chase down some unknown man and rip him apart because Lucy had naughty thoughts about him.

"You're safe in Stillwater." *You're safe with me.* Damian turned and walked out of the office. Despite the distance, he caught her last words.

"I know," she whispered.

Damian gripped the cold steering wheel of his SUV and pushed against the smooth leather of the seat to alleviate the tension knotting his back. Canvassing had yielded no leads, and with little information to go on, this case wouldn't be easy to close quickly. Muscles tense, he itched to stalk into the coffee shop and tell Lucy to go home and sleep. Even if it was only the afternoon. She worked too hard. She could've easily hired another employee or a business manager by now, but she was too stubborn to delegate.

He understood why Lucy disliked him when his words came out all wrong, but now it seemed it didn't matter what he said or did. Helping her out last year made no difference, either. Apparently, he'd dug a hole so deep, he'd never find his way out.

That shouldn't bother him. There were plenty of other women in Stillwater. Plenty of interested women. He'd even forced himself to go on a few dates, but quickly lost interest.

And as always, his mind drifted to Lucy. Gloriously naked with the moonlight bathing her full breasts, narrow waist and haughty expression.

Why yes, he did dare to eat her hare.

If only he'd kept his mouth shut. He should have taken her into his arms that night to feed a different hunger; instead, all sorts of stupid tumbled out of his mouth.

"Are you even listening to me?" Mateo's voice scolded him over the phone.

"Not really."

"This could be related to the flower shop incident."

Damian nodded even though Mateo couldn't see him. "Vandalism in Stillwater is rare enough. Two incidents this close together? They have to be related. Did you want to check in with Mrs. Bee?"

Mateo grunted and hung up. Guess that was a yes. Cranky bastard.

The wind whistled against his vehicle while he remained cocooned in the heated interior. Just because he could saunter around in the buff in the middle of winter didn't mean he always wanted to.

Damian returned to watching the coffee shop. He'd left Lucy hours ago and itched to march back in and stake out some territory amongst the pedestal tables and gossiping clientele. Maybe the criminal would return on his watch. He twirled a pen above an empty page in his notepad. After the canvassing came up empty, he needed to find a new approach for the investigation. He was missing something.

A familiar black-haired beauty sauntered down the sidewalk and Damian cringed. Arabia Jensen from the Silverwind Conspiracy. A vagabond by nature, she made a living by performing readings for superstitious clientele and skirting the law.

He slid lower in his seat. He'd gone on one date with her. One. He knew why he'd done it—a pitiful attempt to forget Lucy—but he hadn't figured out Arabia's motives. At first, he thought the raven shifter was genuinely interested, but her indifference became abundantly clear as the date progressed. What was she after?

Dressed in leather pants and boots with sparkling heels, Arabia swung a small bag in her hand, a smug smile splayed across her face. She glanced across the street and their gazes met. He stiffened. His pen stopped.

Arabia's smile broadened and she waggled her fingers.

Damian's scalp prickled and his griffin surged up, pressing hard against his skin. He'd met enough ravenborn to practice extreme caution wherever and whenever they were involved. Sure, Arabia and he ended on amicable terms, but he never called her back for a second date. Neither did he get the impression she wanted one or harbored any ill-will toward him. But now, her roguish smile and twinkling gaze spoke of plotting.

And a ravenborn plotting always led to disaster.

Arabia glanced at the café and waggled her eyebrows.

Damian scowled. Okay, she really was fucking with him. Why?

She blew him a kiss and continued her jaunty walk down the sidewalk. A business man with silver hair and a matching business suit stopped her on the corner.

Damian leaned forward. Without using magic or lowering his window, he couldn't catch anything they said, only a low murmur masked by the wind, distance, and his SUV's insulation. He'd seen this man before. Where? The Clover Club? The coffee shop? The courthouse, maybe. They'd canvassed every building on Main Street.

The stranger was new in town for certain. Normal humans rarely ventured into the town's city limits due to strong aversion spells. If he wasn't a mundane human, though, what the hell was he? He didn't recall picking up a scent wherever he saw this man before.

He was attractive in a coifed mannequin kind of way. Damian's chest tightened. He gripped his pen. Was this the man Lucy thought about earlier? The pen's plastic creaked, threatening to crack. He eased the pressure.

The stranger chatted with Arabia. The afternoon sun shone against his silver hair and overly-white, fake-looking teeth when he smiled.

We should smash him, Hippo growled.

He's not doing anything.

Arabia flipped her long black hair over her shoulder, flashing shiny rings, bracelets, and earrings. A typical ravenborn, she'd bedazzled her whole outfit. Even her hair.

Arabia and the man continued to chat like they knew each

other. She turned and pointed down the street at Rise & Grind, and its boarded window.

Damian's skin grew cold. He cursed. Was this the lead he needed?

Ravens were tricksters and troublemakers by definition and had an unpredictable view on rules. Was Arabia involved in the vandalism? He wouldn't put it past her. But why? To get back at him? Some perceived slight from Lucy? Or was something more nefarious happening here?

Was the man another raven shifter and somehow playing Lucy as a part of this sordid scheme? Was Damian witnessing an actual conspiracy unfold?

After one last look at Lucy's café, he reached forward and turned the key in the ignition. A gust of cool air jostled his vehicle and flung Arabia's hair around. The man shied away from the wind and scowled at the sky. He muttered something to his companion. Arabia nodded and waved toodaloo-style before heading toward more of the shops. The man entered the office building on the corner. Maybe he had a meeting. Damian didn't care. Right now he had to act.

The man's identity would take time to discover without raising any alarms or losing the element of surprise. Arabia on the other hand...

If he hurried, he could get to her place and rig up some surveillance before Arabia headed home. He gripped the steering wheel and eased the SUV away from the curb.

Was he making the right decision?

Yes, you are. Protect Lucy, Hippo chanted.

He'd need more than intuition to get a warrant to plant bugs in a Stillwater citizen's private residence. Even his motives sounded weak when he reviewed them.

Damian sneered. Arabia and he had one thing in common— a fickle interpretation of the law. He abided by the rules, usually, but not when it came to someone he cared about. Not with Lucy at risk.

He pulled up to an empty intersection and stopped for the light.

Sure, setting up cameras and bugs on the ravenborn without a warrant was illegal and wouldn't stand up in court, but his griffin-sense tingled, and it never steered him wrong before. A griffin always knew what transpired in his kingdom.

Besides, it was one thing for that crazy bird to target him, he'd deal with it. As a griffin, he had a powerful grip on the magical streams pouring from the ley lines where the town sat. He could handle whatever Arabia Jensen threw at him. But if she attacked those he cared about—and everyone but Lucy knew who he cared about—that was something else.

If only Damian could bubble wrap Lucy.

Images of Lucy naked in the moonlight coursed through his mind again.

"Dammit!" He tightened his grip on the steering wheel and forged ahead.

He'd do anything he could to protect Lucy, even if she wanted nothing to do with him. Mateo was right. He had it bad.

And he didn't even have the common sense to be scared.

CHAPTER THREE

ALL CHAINED UP WITH NOWHERE TO GO

Drained from hastily installing surveillance equipment, Damian navigated the SUV around the corner onto Main Street. The tires slid out and the vehicle spun. He gripped the steering wheel, righted the SUV and cursed. This time of year always set him on edge. One, he preferred flying to driving mundane human creations. Two, the weather at this time of year never decided whether it wanted to spit freezing rain, slush or snow, so at any given moment, it showered the residents of Stillwater with whatever fit its fancy.

Weather isn't a person, you know, Hippo piped up.

After he bugged Arabia's cabin, he'd gone home to shower and washed away all traces of her scent. He made some calls and assigned several officers on investigative duty to unearth all the visitors in town. Technically, he had more serious cases to pursue and didn't have the time to stakeout a café for a broken window, but that wouldn't stop him from driving by at every available opportunity to ensure no further vandalism occurred.

Wow, you really do want Lucy. You're voluntarily driving. His griffin chuckled.

And you don't?

Lucy's the best, Hippo agreed.

His griffin rarely shut up about the lynx shifter. They had it bad, and they both knew it. Damian continued to drive toward Rise & Grind. His windshield wipers moved hypnotically to clear the light splattering of slush and rain.

A blur of fur caught his eye. *No.*

Mmmm, yes. Hippo perked up.

Damian skidded the vehicle to a halt and threw open the door. He jumped out. "Lucy!"

A lynx with a beautiful, full winter coat, turned and blinked at him. Female lynx normally weighed anywhere from eleven to thirty pounds, but as a shifter morphing from a human woman's body, Lucy was larger. Weighing roughly sixty pounds and standing around thirty inches tall, she'd dwarf her cousins. The sight of her stole his breath away.

"I thought I told you not to investigate on your own?" he scolded.

The lynx barked at him. The chatter of a lynx sounded eerily close to the annoying dog next door when left alone for too long.

"You're not going after the vandal on your own."

She hissed at him—a much lower and deadlier sound than before. Her ears pinned back and her muscles tensed.

The hairs on his arms stood up. She had no reason to defend her territory against him, but why couldn't she admit he was right? "I'm serious."

So was she, it seemed. She hissed again and turned back to the entrance of her coffee shop, pawing the pavement to rile up the scents.

Stop her! Hippo demanded.

How?

Hippo pushed against his skin, demanding release.

Exactly how is a griffin going to solve this problem? You thought she was food the first time you saw her.

Hippo grumbled, but eased off.

Damian stomped back to his SUV, reached into the cab and grabbed the leash and collar. He always carried a set. Working in a town rife with shifters had taught him a thing or two. He made no attempt to hide his approach as he stomped through slush back to Lucy. Her mischief and mayhem scent curled around him.

Too busy sniffing and sorting through the sensory information near the boarded up window to pay him any attention, he walked right up to her. She continued to ignore him. Typical cat.

"You leave me no choice." He reached down and snapped the collar around her neck.

"Yeeeeeeoooooow!" A murderous scream erupted from the lynx. She whirled around and swatted the air, claws out. Her fangs flashed under the streetlights. Slush sprayed up and splattered his pants.

Damian jumped back, but held onto the chain leash.

She continued her fit while he danced away from each swat. After a number of attempts to part him from his skin, she huffed and sat down.

"Are you done?" Damian asked.

Ooooo boy, you have a death wish, Hippo chortled.

Her sharp gaze pierced at him. Ears back, she hissed again, but she didn't try another attack.

"Lucy. You need to shift."

She blinked at him.

He reached forward and tried the door to Rise & Grind. Locked. He turned back to Lucy. "You shifted at home and ran here, didn't you?"

The cat equivalent of a smirk answered him.

He cursed and looked around. She couldn't shift in the middle of town. She'd end up naked and exposed. He tugged on the leash. "Come on, I'll take you home."

She pulled back and threw her weight toward her butt.

Damian sighed, his shoulders drooping. "I'm not going to leave you out here where someone who's actively targeted your business might be lurking."

She huffed.

"Will you let me take you to Laura? You can shift there." She'd be safe with Laura, and the cougar shifter would have spare clothes.

The lynx blinked again, her enthralling scent spiraling around him, but gave him no clue to what was going on in that brain of hers. After the longest minute of his life, she huffed again and stood up. She turned toward the Clover Club and pulled on the leash.

Damian released a long breath. Having already imagined the horror of trying to shove a sixty pound hellcat intent on shredding his skin to the bone into the back of his SUV, the relief that she agreed to his plan wasn't insignificant.

They walked in silence to the bar next door. Lucy sat at the entrance, calm and cool. She lifted a paw and cleaned her claws.

"Brat."

She stared back, daring him to say more.

He shook his head, backing down from the fight before it started and pushed open the door. Heated air, booze and blues rushed past him.

Hippo growled. So many shifters in one place always set him on edge. After business hours, they flocked to this upscale bar to unwind.

"I really hope you have a good reason for having my friend in a collar," a voice worthy of a late-night rendezvous drawled from the side.

He turned to find Laura scowling at him, her arms folded over her tight plaid shirt and her jean-clad hips cocked to one side. Sleek and beautiful, the owner of the Clover Club radiated confidence and prowess.

"Dear lord save me from sexy felines," he said. He couldn't handle anymore catitude tonight.

Laura smirked. "Well?"

He handed her the end of the leash. "Your friend needs to leave the investigation to the big boys."

Laura scowled. "Or a certain big boy needs to get his head out of his ass."

Lucy growled in agreement, the low hissing call of a pissed off lynx.

A loud thud sounded behind them. They turned in unison. An overweight man in a lumberjack shirt peeled himself off the floor. Beer had sprayed everywhere and some of his drinking buddies cursed at him. He fumbled for the edge of the bar, saggy jeans falling down his backside and granting a view none of them wanted. The man cast his frightened gaze in their direction and staggered to his feet using the bar for support.

Damian sniffed the air. Along with beer and incredibly strong body odor, elk musk wove in the man's scent.

Food, Hippo smacked his lips.

Behave.

"Phil?" Laura leaned around Damian and addressed the stumbling redneck. "You okay?"

"Yeah, yeah." The man waved her off and swayed toward the exit. He opened the door, letting in another whoosh of cold air. "I'll walk it off."

When the door slammed shut, Laura turned to Damian and cast her appraising gaze up and down his body. Though Lucy made the sound that initially scared the elk shifter, his fearful gaze had focused on Damian the entire time he staggered from the bar. "The prey instinct is strong in that one."

It was Damian's turn to flash a toothy smile. Laura had a side-business as a private investigator. If she wanted to know more about him, she'd have to hustle that butt of hers and find out for her goddamned self.

"So you only leashed Lucy to stop her from investigating the damage to her territory and subject her to your chauvinistic views?"

"Yes." Wait a minute. "What? No."

She rose an eyebrow.

He wisely clamped his mouth shut.

"Shame. I'd hoped something kinky was going on." She gave the leash a gentle tug toward the back of the bar. "I have clothes for Lucy in the back. You may go now."

Knowing when he was outnumbered, outclassed and dismissed, he grunted a goodbye and left. Hippo pressed against his skin, nudging his brain.

Yeah, buddy. We'll hunt. He had to do something to run off this extra steam and agitation.

CHAPTER FOUR

A HUNTING WE WILL GO

L ucy followed Laura to her office in the back. Her feet padded feather-light against the floor amongst the loud patrons yammering about their days over cold beer. The door closed, cutting off the babble and the saturated smell of booze.

Laura kneeled and pulled off the collar. "Do I want to know why the handsome Damian Charming has you all leashed up?"

Technically, Laura already knew Damian's motives, but a cynic at heart, the cougar shifter rarely took a man at his word. Lucy bonked her forehead against Laura's.

Her friend laughed and straightened. She tossed the leash and collar on her desk and reached over to pull clothes from the nearby shelf. They smelled of clean-linen dryer sheets. "I don't believe for one second he told the whole truth. You better watch out for that one, Luce. He's hiding something."

Lucy blinked at her friend.

"These will be too long for you, my vertically-challenged friend," she said, tossing the sweatpants and T-shirt onto her office chair. "But they'll cover the important bits. You can keep your kinky straps. I'll see you outside."

Seconds after Laura left and closed the door quietly behind her, Lucy shifted. She hadn't really thought her actions through, but how was she to guess Damian would charge over, scold her like a misbehaving child and leash her like a troublesome stray? If he hadn't caught her sniffing around—quite literally—she would've loped back to her house and no one would have been the wiser.

Damian hinted she might be in danger. Was she? Surely she'd be better off handling the situation in her lynx form than her human one. When she was a lynx, the world around her made more sense, her body moved on instinct and she didn't have to think to defend herself. As a human, she couldn't claim such capabilities.

An image of a woman with her face, about fifteen years older than Lucy's current age flashed through her memory. Green eyes crinkled with laughter. A soft mouth and a tender expression. Mom. A familiar pain stabbed Lucy's heart. Mom had been in lynx form when she was killed.

Lucy shivered and pulled on the sweat pants. Laura was right, they were too long. No one else had giraffe legs like that woman. Lucy pulled the drawstring as tightly as possible and folded the waistband over multiple times. Once she rolled up both legs, she pulled on the starchy T-shirt. The hard cotton chaffed against her nipples, but as Laura said, the important bits were covered.

She grabbed the leash and collar and looped the leash so she could carry the set without anything dragging. With a deep breath, she pulled open the office door. Booze and BO hit her face. She padded over to the counter, bare feet slapping against sticky flooring. *Don't think about it. Don't think about it.*

We'll scrub those feet when we get home, Whispurr piped up.

She climbed onto a barstool and plonked the leash and

collar on the smooth surface of the bar. When Laura finished serving other customers along the bar, she wordlessly poured a pint of beer and slid the glass on the counter to Lucy. "I heard you had a little window problem."

"Nothing I can't handle." She straightened.

"Like Damian's going to let you take care of this yourself."

"What's that supposed to mean?"

"You saw him. He won't even let you catch a scent of the criminal. That's what you were doing, was it not?"

Lucy nodded, not that her heightened senses helped any. Too many people frequented the sidewalk on a daily basis for her to pick up anything helpful. "He said the vandal might be lurking around waiting to do more damage or even hurt me."

Laura's shrewd green gaze narrowed. "He might be right. We don't know why someone targeted your business, yet."

Lucy sighed and took a long sip of cold beer. It coated her tongue and cooled her throat as she swallowed.

"I can look into it if you want." Laura examined her nails.

"Thanks, but I'll handle this."

Laura nodded. "There's nothing wrong with wanting to protect what is yours. I know how fiercely territorial you are."

Lucy laughed. The first time they met they were in their respective feline forms and had a major spat over a large section of forest. They sorted it out. "But?"

"Damian has a point. You might be in danger. There's also nothing wrong with accepting help. He'll take care of it. You know he will."

"Yeah, but this is *mine*."

Laura pulled a rag from behind the bar and wiped the counter. She didn't comment. Rowdy customers at the other end of the bar called for shots.

Geez, it was Monday night.

Once Laura finished serving them, she wandered back to Lucy, cleaning the bar and casting serious side-eye her way.

"Have you figured out what Damian is yet?"

Not this again. Laura had a keen nose for trouble and knew Damian hid something. Lucy couldn't lie to her friend even if she wanted, but revealing Damian's secret felt like a betrayal. She kept her mouth clamped shut and shrugged.

"I could find out for you..." Laura purred.

Lucy laughed. It wasn't that Laura had romantic interest in Damian, Laura couldn't stand not knowing things. "For me or for yourself?"

Laura flashed a wicked grin and poured another beer. She held it out.

Lucy clinked her glass against Laura's. "Curiosity killed the cat, you know."

They both grinned and drank.

"You going home after this?" Laura asked, whisking away Lucy's empty pint.

"No. I'm still pent up and my lynx is restless. I'm going to hunt. Want to go kill some rabbits?" The offer surprised her. Normally, she preferred to hunt alone. They both did.

Shock flashed through Laura's expression. Her features softened, and then something dark worked its way into her gaze. It was like watching a mood stone change color.

"No, thanks, Luce," Laura said. "I appreciate the invitation. I really do. But I need to work off a different kind of energy."

Well, now. Not much she could say to that. Lucy slipped from her stool, sliding the leash and collar off the table. She mock saluted her friend. "I'll catch you later then."

Laura winked. "Show those bunnies no mercy."

"Never!"

Soft wind rippled through Lucy's fur like a gentle lover's caress. After a long shift at the shop, the vandalism and that...man...she needed to feel her paws dig into the snow-dusted soil and weave through the dancing trees.

The double shifting left her nerves frayed, but nothing a cold night wouldn't fix. Scents of rabbits nearby drifted on the breeze. Lucy huffed. Not snowshoe hare like she preferred. Not like *home*. She missed many things after she left—the cold bite of Canadian air before snowfall, paws sinking deep into fresh powder, people knowing the correct term for a winter hat was toque, not beanie, and chasing white hares with a flurry of feet kicking up snow.

The local bunnies in Stillwater would have to do. She stalked around the trees, padded paws pressing the forest floor. The wind continued to tease her ear tuffs.

Her mom had taught her how to hunt as a kit. With an absentee father, Lucy was left with no one after the hunting accident that claimed her mom's life. With nothing more to lose except solitude and painful memories, Lucy headed to Stillwater for a fresh start.

Branches snapped downwind. Probably a deer. Her ears pinged forward. She didn't hunt larger game, but taking down a small doe tonight might assuage some of the heartache and restlessness. She changed direction and loped through the snow. She weaved around thick tree trunks. Her heart beat in unison with the padding of her paws. She loved how her feline body moved in tune with the trees and rhythm of the land. The cold air burned her nose. She pressed on, pushing her lynx form faster than usual, and burst through the brush.

Wings. Gold. Large. Predator.

She flung her paws forward and skidded to a halt. Snow, now deeper, sprayed up, showering the large griffin with a blanket of white powder. His magical scent curled around her. Technically, to her lynx nose, he smelled of lion musk and faintly of eagle, but there was so much more wound into his very male essence. She never smelled anything like Damian.

In human form, the scent lingered, subtly, but fully shifted, the aroma was overwhelming, much like the rest of him. Magic, ethereal essence, unicorns and rainbows, all wrapped up in one olfactory punch, but without the pretty pink bow. Instead, his scent carried a warning of danger—the instinctive knowledge he was a deadly, magical predator with ruthless cunning. A promise of his intent, either on the battleground or in the bedroom.

She backpedaled rapidly, legs flailing under her while she ran in one place. There was no point, Damian turned around and the full magnificence of his griffin form stared down at her. Lightning danced in his gaze. With the head, wings and talons of a mighty eagle and the body, back legs and tail of a lion, the majestic subject of Greek and Roman myths radiated power and authority.

Lucy had caved and researched griffins after their last run-in and a glass or five of wine.

According to legend, eagles were considered the king of birds, and lions of beasts, making the griffin the king of all creatures.

No wonder the man had a superiority complex and radiated arrogance.

Did he want to rule her?

Part of her squealed with delight, while the rest of Lucy groaned. Even her internal dialogue wanted a piece of him.

Her gut twisted. When had she fallen for this arrogant jerk? How much longer could she wear the shield of his condescension as protection against what her heart desired? She'd truly make an ass out of herself, too. He would never slum it with a lowly lynx.

He cocked his head, but his piercing eagle gaze held no surprise, only calculation.

She scowled, which in lynx form translated to baring her teeth.

Damian's wings snapped out and refolded against his back.

37

She flinched. Had she intruded on some superior majestic mythological shifter ceremony? She continued to back up, but she refused to cower or drop her gaze.

The air around Damian rushed around his tall frame in a frenzied whirlwind and shimmered. Lightning shot through the sky. When had it started to storm?

Lucy froze.

Weak beams of moonlight from the waning crescent above streamed through the sparkling air. No bone snapping, tissue tearing, fluid oozing grotesque change like hers. With a blast of his heavenly scent, the magical mist dissipated to reveal Damian.

Naked Damian.

Well, naked except the silver rings he always wore. Other than the essence shielding one, she had no idea what the rest of the rings did. With a surname of "Charming," though, she could hazard a guess. She must be immune to his spells.

She snuck another look at naked Damian. Broad shoulders, powerful chest tapering to a narrow waist. An impressive griffin tattoo on his chest distracted her for two seconds before her gaze drifted down. He was perfection. Just like the first time. Maybe she'd wasn't as immune to his "charms" as she would like. She hoped her imagination had exaggerated his body's powerful composition.

Nope.

Is that why she craved affection from him instead of derision?

She pawed the dirt and looked away. If only the answer to that question was yes. She could hate-bang an attractive man, but that's not what drew her to the detective.

She parked her butt on the cold snow and waited. Slinking away now wasn't an option.

"You should be sleeping," Damian said. With confident steps, he closed the distance, pale skin with no hint of a blush.

"Why are you out hunting?"

Why are *you* out hunting, she wanted to ask. She wasn't the only one who worked long hours. Her gaze drifted down again. He had no reason to blush and a large reason for confidence. Huge reason.

He sat on the ground beside her. His thigh less than a foot away. Their position gave them a clear view of the moon, a glowing sliver bathing them in light. Not that she was looking at the moon.

"I'm sorry someone damaged the coffee shop," he said. "I know how much it means to you."

Did he expect her to change to human and sit beside him for a deep conversation while naked? Not happening. She might be comfortable in her body, but she didn't trust her own intentions. She had no wish for rejection tonight. No, thank you.

"I'm also sorry for how I spoke to you."

Lucy stiffened. What? An apology from the king of all creatures? She glanced over, but Damian watched the moon instead of her.

"It seems I never say the right thing."

He said all sorts of right things tonight. Her body hummed with awareness. She knew exactly how much space separated them. Maybe she should shift to human and press her naked body against his?

He'd brush her off like unwanted dirt. Unease rippled down her coat. Instead of trying to proposition the hunk of man beside her, she settled into the snow, resigned to the idea she'd have to continue hating the detective because he'd never accept her love.

CHAPTER FIVE

HASTY RETREATS

Tuesday, November 6th

Damian sat back in the leather chair and swallowed the coffee in a large gulp. Afternoon sun streamed in the one intact window to the Rise & Grind and bathed his partner in light while he remained in the dark.

Hippo snorted. *Physically and figuratively.*

Normally, he enjoyed his latté from the Rise & Grind almost as much as the unimpeded views of Lucy at work, but not today. The coffee tasted fine, but it sat wrong and it had nothing to do with the product. Not only had someone attacked Lucy's workplace yesterday, but he'd spent the last hour trying to engage his moody partner in conversation. He abandoned all attempts at discussing their cases after one-word replies, and frankly, Mateo started to piss him off. He'd been distant and cold lately, but refused to elaborate on what exactly was up his ass.

"How's your little sister doing in college?" Damian asked.

"Seems happy. Made some friends." Mateo shifted in his seat and stared at the table.

Damian squeezed his empty cup. The lid popped off. Damian grunted and swooped it off the floor. "I bet she misses you. It's hard to relocate to a new place."

Mateo glared daggers at him.

Well, attempt twenty-three was also unsuccessful. What was his problem? Mateo was the more stable one in this partnership.

"Yeah," Mateo said, tone venomous. "Especially when you don't have someone to look out for you. You know, find an apartment, a vacant spot for your business, order furniture. Hell, even set up bank accounts."

Shit. They weren't talking about his sister anymore. How did Mateo find out he helped Kiera? Damian agreed to help the bear shifter relocate to Stillwater for a friend. He would've told Mateo, but his friend swore Damian to secrecy. He glanced at his partner.

Still daggers.

This was *Mateo*. He couldn't lie to his partner, but how much should he share?

"I see those wheels turning, Damian. Right about now you're trying to figure how much to tell me." Mateo crossed his arms. He always did that when he knew he was right. "I suggest everything."

"This has to stay between the two of us. Creighton doesn't want Kiera to know."

Mateo nodded once, his face still a mask simmering with anger. "Who is Creighton?"

"He's the head of Kiera's bear shifter sleuth in Scotland." Damian placed his empty cup on the table between them and shoved the errant lid inside.

Mateo waited.

"Apparently, Kiera hooked up with an 'ordinary' who dealt

drugs. When she found his stash in her house, she turned them over to Creighton. Some bad things went down and he wanted her out of the country. Creighton and I met a few years ago and he contacted me for help. She's gone through some shit. He wanted to make this move easy for her." He shrugged. "That's all there is to it."

He hadn't left out anything, yet Mateo's glower remained unaltered. He sat stiffly in the chair across from Damian, the subtle twitch of his right eye the only movement. What the hell? Damian did something nice, and when confronted about it, told the fucking truth. Why was Mateo pissed off about Damian helping Keira?

"Wait." Damion glanced around to the empty tables neighboring their own before leaning toward Mateo. "Is this what's had your chonies in knots these last few weeks? Have you got a thing for her?"

This time Mateo shrugged. "Maybe."

Damian's face nearly split in two with his grin. Mateo's glare quickly snuffed the joy out of his smile, though, and Damian scrunched his face, trying to hide it. From Mateo's dark look, he was unsuccessful. Damian picked up his cup to conceal his expression. The smell of old coffee filled his nose. Crap. He'd already finished it and the lid was stuffed inside. He put the cup down again.

Mateo's scowl slipped and he unfolded his arms to glance at his watch. "I've got to go. I'll call you later to discuss our cases."

Damian nodded and leaned back in the chair while his partner made a quick escape. He'd never seen Mateo so unsettled. The door opened and closed quickly with Mateo's exit and sent a gust of cool winter air into the shop.

"You look like the cat who got in the cream."

Lucy's singsong voice pulled his attention away from his partner's departure. He turned in his chair and looked up at the lynx shifter. She stood by Mateo's vacant chair in the same stream of sunlight. Tight jeans clung to her athletic legs, and she wore a large knit sweater that covered the curves he longed to explore. Her tawny hair shone with warm hues of brown, red and gold, and her honey eyes looked so inviting he could melt in her gaze.

Mmmmmm, Hippo perked up.

When their gazes met, her cheeks flushed and she looked away. The scent of arousal lifted from her skin.

Damian straightened in his seat. Was she thinking about him? She'd seen him naked last night. Was she recalling the details? Did she visualize him now with her without clothes?

When she'd almost physically run into him, he'd smelled her shock and tasted her fear in the air. It rankled his feathers. He'd shifted to human form to put her at ease even though he had no clothes with him. He smiled, recalling how they'd sat in amicable silence watching the moon. She might bristle and act put out by his presence, but maybe, just maybe, she didn't hate him as much as he thought.

Lucy swiped the used cups off the table and dropped them in a gray bin, still not meeting his eyes. The red of her cheeks easing away to a delicate shade of rose. "Am I too optimistic in hoping that smug smile is from figuring out who's responsible for damaging my property?"

"Unfortunately, yes," Damian said. "I wish I had news for you."

"Do you have anything for me?"

Yeah, Hippo cackled. *A giant—*

He shut the lid on his griffin's grating voice.

Hippo pushed it back open. *Tip, I was going to say tip.*

Sure you were. Be quiet, beast. I'm trying to weave some magic here.

Not literally, of course. Even if he possessed that kind of magic, he'd never spell Lucy into liking him. Instead, he'd have to rely on his questionable charm. He sat forward. "What would you like?"

Surprise flashed across Lucy's face. The pink returned, creeping up her neck to spread across her cheeks. "Uhh..."

He rested his forearm on the table. Was she having more dirty thoughts? Maybe she wasn't a lynx so much as a little minx.

"My window replaced, obviously," she stammered.

"Is that what they're calling it these days?"

"Uhh..." The pink deepened to a nice red.

My, my, someone is flustered. Did her cheeks flush like that when she came? Would she moan his name with that sultry voice of hers?

"Well, I already boarded your *window*. Would you like me to replace it, too?" he asked.

If Lucy was in her lynx form, she would've shook her fur coat like a wet dog. In her human skin, she shook her head, her wavy mane brushing her face as it bobbed back and forth.

"Absolutely not." Lucy pulled herself straighter, as if she magically replaced her spine with rebar. "The insurance company will be here within the next day or two to *replace* the window. Professionally."

"They might be professional, but I'm a pro."

"At replacing windows?"

"Sure."

She clutched the gray bin to her chest, spun on her heel and walked back to the counter where a small line had accumulated—nothing Tanner couldn't handle on his own—without a word.

Damian settled back in his seat. That was twice in one sitting someone had beat a hasty retreat from his presence. Mateo's escape amused him, but Lucy's...

Lucy's gave him hope.

CHAPTER SIX

HEX APPEAL

Wednesday Evening, November 7th

Damian wrenched the coffee shop door open. The cold air laden with snow followed him into the heated cocoon of coffee-scented space with soft music gently playing over the speakers. This close to closing, he'd expected the place to be empty, but another customer lingered.

Lucy straightened from the display case with a white rag and cleaning spray in one hand. A simple gray T-shirt clung to her curves and skinny jeans showed off her athletic legs. Damn.

Tension released from his shoulders. After repeated reports of vandalism on the block, he worried about her. Instinctively, he knew she was okay because she would've called if something had happened, but his skin itched all day to see her, or at least text her. He resisted. Barely. But after a long shift, he needed to see her and confirm with his own eyes she was safe.

"Hey, Damian." Lucy set the cleaning supplies on the

counter. "Is everything okay?"

He snuffed the potent need to stalk over and take her in his arms. Instead, his gaze drifted to the other late night patron.

The business man who'd spoken to Arabia a couple of days ago stood from a plastic chair by one of the pedestal tables. He straightened his tie. Annoyance flashed across his expression.

Damian paused. Was this guy lingering at closing time for Lucy? This was the third time he'd seen the man in a couple of days—three more times than he'd like. The businessman held himself with authority and buttoned his suit jacket. His silver gray hair sparkled under the interior lights like a fucking Christmas ornament.

The guy had money. A lot of it if his shiny watch was any indicator. Damian had money, too, but flashing it around wouldn't impress Lucy.

"Damian?" Lucy tilted her head, still waiting for an answer.

"There's been another incident. I wanted to check in with you."

Her eyebrows rose. "Careful, Detective. I might start to think you really do worry."

"I wanted to ensure nothing more happened here and whether you saw anything suspicious this evening."

Coward. Hippo gathered their griffin nature and coiled around his neck, threatening to choke him.

Lucy smirked. "It's well past eight now anyway. Let me close up."

The stranger's mouth pinched in before he smoothed his expression and turned to Lucy. "Goodnight. Thank you for the coffee."

Lucy beamed at the businessman, her smile open and genuine.

Damian narrowed his eyes.

The man left his claimed territory, ignoring the empty mug on the table, and brushed past Damian to leave the café. A wake of expensive cologne trailed behind him. No raven scent. No animal scent at all. Nothing remotely hinting of supernatural powers.

Damian wanted to punch him, but the urge was completely irrational. The businessman had done nothing to Damian except talk to Lucy.

And Arabia.

Both women were beautiful. Maybe the guy was a helpless flirt, not a co-conspirator for vandalism. He certainly wasn't a shifter. Damian groaned internally. One of these theories made sense, the other was a stretch. According to the law of parsimony, the simplest solution was often the right one.

In other words, Damian was an idiot.

Sadly, this wasn't and wouldn't be the only time he overreacted where Lucy was involved. Damian tensed, his muscles demanding action. He'd fucked up. His jealousy of this guy and his suspicion of Arabia had lead him to the land of stupid. He'd have to remove the surveillance equipment from the raven shifter's cabin before anyone found out about his transgression.

The door closed behind the businessman leaving Damian alone with Lucy in the soft glow and warmth of the café. *Relax. Fix this little procedural error later.*

He jerked his thumb at the café's entrance. "New regular?"

Lucy shrugged and picked up the mugs left on a nearby table. "I hope so. He said he's looking into opening a business in town and buys a lot of coffee."

"What kind of business?"

She shrugged again, dishes in hand. "Didn't say."

Damian nodded, but his mind growled. That *businessman* had more than business on his mind. He reached over and grabbed two discarded takeaway cups left on a table and threw them in the nearby trash. "Think he could be the vandal?"

Lucy laughed and placed the dishes in a bin and turned to

him. Her laughter faltered. "Oh. You're serious."

"The vandalism isn't characteristic of a Stillwater citizen."

"And you think it fits a slick businessman from the city?"

He grumbled. What the hell did she mean by slick? Did women consider this a good or bad trait in a man?

"I don't think that man's picked up a brick in his life."

"I didn't realize I interrupted you revelling in his soft pansy hands."

Lucy rolled her eyes. "I shook his hand. It was soft."

Damian took a deep breath. His griffin surged up. If he left now, he could track the man and...and what? Smite him for touching Lucy? He scowled.

"Careful. Your face might stay scrunched like that."

"He could've paid someone to do it." He wove around the tables and plucked the remaining cups left on the tables. He walked them over to Lucy and leaned forward to gently place them in the bin. His face came dangerously close to Lucy's. Her scent coiled around him, full of velvety spice. He could bask in her presence all day.

Lucy stepped back, her chest moving quickly with little short breaths. She hoisted the bin of dishes and moved them to the backroom. She called over her shoulder as she left his sight. "Now you really are fucking with me."

Not the kind of fucking he had in mind.

Lucy returned, pushing through the swinging doors. "Seriously. I think we all would've noticed evil henchmen lurking around."

"They hardly wear nametags."

She crossed her arms.

"Evil henchmen don't announce themselves. I said vandalism didn't fit Stillwater, not that there wasn't a crime element."

"You said things were slow."

"Slow, not non-existent."

"So we have evil henchmen?" She clapped her hands and bounced. "Can I meet one?"

Damian cursed and looked at the ceiling. If he watched her bounce anymore, he'd lose control.

"Do they have rough hands? Can I touch one?"

"Absolutely not!"

"Party pooper." Lucy stopped clapping. "Let me lock up. I know you have more questions for me and this way you can interrogate me without any interruptions."

"Interrogate?" He smiled. He'd love to do so much more.

Lucy snorted. "Question a potential witness then. You and Mateo certainly have the good cop, bad cop routine down."

"Your smile indicates you like my questioning," he said.

Lucy faltered and her eyes widened.

He shrugged, but inside he cursed. His heart's desire stood eight feet away, turning off an open sign and he was incapable of having anything other than stupid tumble from his mouth.

Rejection was always a possibility, but not enough of a deterrent to stop him from going after what he wanted if he thought his affection might be welcomed.

The main problem was he wanted Lucy too much. Even if she was attracted to him, and they formed a relationship, Damian didn't trust himself to hold back. And if he bonded with her, and her momentary passion turned to indifference, he'd be alone forever. The act of bonding was irreversible and lasted a lifetime for griffins. He couldn't risk it.

Lucy flicked off the lights, leaving the soft glow of the display case and the kitchen lights to illuminate the café. She waved at him to follow her and walked past the counter to the back room. The sweet smells of sugar, vanilla and cinnamon flooded his senses as he joined her in the kitchen. The door swung shut behind him, trapping them in the smaller space.

An oven and counter occupied one side, shelves packed with stock on the other, and metallic doors faced him with a large island taking up the center of the room. The bin of dirty dishes sat by an industrial-sized sink and commercial dishwasher. The kitchen was larger than he expected.

"I've never been back here," he said.

Lucy nodded and leaned against the island. She suddenly looked exhausted. "The kitchen kind of sold this location to me. I walked in here and knew I had to have this place."

"Helps to have the court house across the street."

"Criminals and their lawyers need caffeine, too." Her smile spread, growing a little shrewder. She might have the rest of the town fooled, presenting the sweet side of her personality, but he'd seen enough glimpses of her wickedness over the years. A smart, calculating businesswoman saw this once floundering café and turned it into a thriving enterprise.

"What do you need?" she glanced at the clock. "Not that I don't mind answering your questions, but it's almost nine and I hoped for an early night."

"Yeah, sure thing, Luce." He pulled out his notepad and froze. Magical whispers in the wind trickled through the air.

Pray, hear my words, Ceridwen, Mother of Magic...

A shiver ran along his spine. Someone was working potent magic tonight. As a griffin, he was mostly immune to magic and the dabbling of low level wielders, but this packed a serious punch. He shook the spell off.

The light in the kitchen flared. His heart contracted. He narrowed his eyes.

Lucy swayed. She lifted a hand to her forehead as if to take her own temperature. Her mouth parted.

"You okay?" he asked.

"Yeah." She nodded, tawny hair flowing past her smooth cheeks. Her sweet scent remained unchanged. Whatever swept through the room left her unscathed as well. "Let the interrogation begin."

He grinned. "I thought you were looking forward to my

questions."

"I am, but that's not exactly what I want to be doing right now." Heat flashed through her honey gaze.

He widened his stance. As a shifter, he was a master at reading body language. She couldn't possible mean...No. His breath caught. She hated him, didn't she? He couldn't possible hope...

He never pursued her because her dislike for him was evident. Although he'd felt and heard her sincere gratitude for helping with her crazy father, he also sensed her embarrassment. The scent always spiraled around her when he saw her.

Magic wrapped around him in a sheath and nudged him forward. *You want her*, it pulsed. *Here she is within arm's reach.*

She wasn't a griffin.

The magic hummed. No. That didn't matter. It never mattered. Lucy was loyal. Fierce. *Mine.*

"What would you rather be doing?" he growled.

"You."

Lucy's brain clambered to make sense of the words coming out of her mouth. She smoothed her hands down the side of her cotton shirt. Either that or she'd splay them against Damian's broad chest. He stood statue-still in front of her, gaze flashing under the soft café lighting.

Had she really just said that? Had she really told the griffin how she truly felt? If she bolted now, could she outrun the humiliation?

How could she fix this? How could she take this—?

A soothing wave of reassurance coated her skin. It would be okay. He needed to hear the truth.

It's about time, Whispurr scoffed.

"Me?" Damian's dark brows shot up. "I thought you hated me."

Tension slid from her body, replaced with languid confidence.

"Oh, your arrogance pisses me off, but I've never hated you."

He took a menacing step forward. His nostrils flared. He scented the air. She smelled it, too. Her lust. Her desire...and his? Her breath caught. Her heart hammered. Did he feel the same way?

"What do you feel for me then? If not hatred?"

She gulped. She couldn't possibly tell him her heart's desire. He'd reject her and the mortification would drown her.

Then she might truly hate him.

"Luce?"

Her nickname on his tongue sent shivers racing down her body. His lion and eagle scent curled around her, along with a heady mix of lust.

"What do you feel?" He moved closer, predator stalking prey. His gaze intense, stripped of his shielding and glamour. Fierce and fiery raw emotion stared back at her.

"I like you," she whispered.

"Like?" He leaned down and cocked his head.

"Maybe more."

"Maybe more?" he murmured. His gaze flicked to her lips.

Her heart convulsed. Did his griffin eyes see straight into her heart? Her soul? Did he know she craved him more than caffeine and sugar? Combined? That her blood pulsed with the promise she saw in his intense gaze.

"Your heart is racing," he said.

"So is yours."

He smiled. A tender smile. She'd never seen anything but sharp angles and attitude from him. He reached out. His hand hesitated inches from her face. "Is this what you want?"

She nodded and slid her hands up his chest, his sweater soft under her fingers.

He shivered, but still held back, worry knotting his brow. His breathing slowed to match hers.

She licked her dry lips, the wait agonizing. Why was he concerned? What was she missing? Did he not want her? She stiffened. Oh no, please, not that.

Before she could snatch her hands back, he pulled her in and crushed his mouth against hers. A hungry kiss, full of longing and lust. He tasted of coffee and salacious promises.

Yes! Whispurr crooned.

Yes, she agreed, melting into Damian's kiss.

She'd lied to herself for years. First telling herself she held back out of embarrassment and shame, then anger, but if she was truly honest, she held back because she didn't believe she was worthy and thought Damian believed the same.

This kiss though. This kiss told her a different story entirely.

She molded into the heat of his arms, corded with muscle. He held her against the strength of his chest. Her breasts smashed against his hard body. His magic flowed out and coated her skin. Thick and heavy, the potent energy stroked her. Damien's mouth consumed hers, tasting and teasing, lips soft and devilish.

She slid her hands underneath his shirt and sweater, running her fingers along the smooth muscles of his back. A low growl rumbled from his throat. He pulled back and caught the hem of her shirt. His gaze, now blazing like a summer thunderstorm, raked over her body.

Her breath caught at the lust written in his intense expression. He pulled her shirt off. The cotton fabric whispered against the floor where he dropped it. Just when she thought he couldn't possibly look at her with more desire, raw need flashed across his gaze.

Heat flushed her skin. Aching need throbbed between her legs. She wanted him. She needed him. Here. Now.

She pulled his shirt and sweater off in a single motion. The harsh kitchen lights danced on his muscular chest, bringing to life the large griffin tattoo splayed over his left pec. Over his heart. She ran her fingers along the outline.

Damian whisked her hands away and tugged at her belt. His lips explored her skin. He shimmied her jeans down. The belt buckle clanked on the stone floor.

She attacked his pants. Why couldn't he be naked already?

In seconds, he was naked and she was in his arms. His hands slipped down her back. His mouth claimed hers again. The tease gone. Instead, he kissed her as if every touch expressed his heart. She arched against him, splaying her naked skin along his. He growled against her mouth. His hands gripped her butt and lifted her onto the kitchen island, sliding her along the countertop. She wrapped her legs around his solid torso, rippled with muscle.

His lips moved along her neck, nipping, sucking, and kissing. A male groan vibrated against her skin. His magic caressed her and he kneaded one breast with his hand while teasing the other with his tongue. Need pooled low in her belly.

They were going to have sex. Right now. Right here. In her kitchen and she didn't care. She wanted him inside her, filling her, moving within her and easing this unbearable ache.

His lips left her breasts and traveled over her stomach and down her body. His mouth clamped on her and the world around her disappeared as he devoured her.

Lucy dropped her head back, shutting her eyes against the glow of the kitchen lights, and surrendered to the pleasure Damian's mouth provided. Tingling delight flooded her body, warmth pressed against her skin. A low moan filled the room. Her moan, she realized.

The exquisite pressure built and built until it broke,

splintering across her skin and within her body, flowing from her core to the tips of her fingers and toes. She cried out, the release almost unbearable.

Without giving her a chance to recover, Damian stood, gripped her hips and impaled her. Sheathed within, his thick shaft filled her. The last throes of her orgasm gripped him.

Oh my god, yes.

His fingers dug into her hips. He growled, gaze wild. His expression fierce and intense, focused on her. When the orgasm relented, he slowly withdrew, sliding out with delicious pressure. She was so wet. The need for him came crashing back. What was he doing? Why wasn't he giving her more? He pulled almost all the way out. She cried out, "No."

He slammed back in. Thick and long, he stretched her. He pumped his hips, thrusting again and again into her heat, stroking the need and ache all over again. She was on fire, and he was the fuel.

He clutched the back of her head, fingers snagging the hair at the base of her skull and pulled her in for another dizzying kiss. His pace unrelenting, he continued to drive into her, claiming her with his body and mouth. His magic wound around her, kneading her breasts, caressing her neck, and sliding along her skin until she couldn't tell where he ended and she began. His magic coated every inch of her body and pulsed, demanding to be let in.

She pulled at the power, drawing in the vibrating energy. The magic soaked into her skin, caressing her nerves and expanding to fill her with Damian's enticing power.

A second orgasm rocked her. She cried out and arched against Damian. More of his magic spread through her body in tune with the waves of orgasmic delight. Pleasure erupted from every cell.

"Mine," Damian growled in her ear. His fingers dug into her skin as he gripped her hips and with one final thrust came inside. His breath fanned her cheek as he rocked against her. His arms slipped around her back and pulled her to him. With coiled muscles, he hauled them onto the solid kitchen island and stretched out beside her. The length of his body heated hers and he ran his hands along sensitive skin. He cloaked them in the warmth of his magic.

She sighed and let the sleep pulling at her languid limbs roll over her. A griffin spooned her. Damian spooned her. She should stay awake and enjoy this moment, but exhaustion dragged down her eyelids and pinned her body to the pillow-soft bed. The tingling remnants of her intense orgasms released all the tension in her muscles. Cocooned in the safety of Damian's arms, she fell asleep.

CHAPTER SEVEN

MAGIC CALLS THE HEART

Two a.m., Thursday morning, Nov 8ᵗʰ

Magic pulsed and rolled through the room. Damian's eyes snapped open. His arms tightened around Lucy. At some point, they'd turned off the lights, and without any windows, only the glow of timers from the nearby appliances illuminated the room. The wind picked up outside and battered the café in the night. The kitchen had long since cooled, but his mate nestled into the heat of his body, saturated in his magic.

After short cat naps, they'd spent the night exploring each other. Need coursed through him again—an ache to claim and slake the lust rampaging through his veins.

She'd accepted his bond and now his energy coiled around them both. The mating process was unfinished, though. He still needed to gift her with his horde to complete the ceremony and keep her safe. It was a simple token, but what might seem like a small gesture and silly tradition to others, meant a great deal to him. To all griffins. After he gifted his mate with the treasure infused with his essence, he could protect Lucy and bond her lifespan to his. Until then, Lucy wouldn't feel the effects of his bond, nor benefit from its power. She'd be vulnerable.

He stroked her smooth arm with his thumb and stared at the kitchen's industrial-style ceiling. The ache knotting in his chest from worry bloomed, giving way to something he'd never felt before. Happy? Was this what it felt like to be truly happy?

Right now, Lucy was safe and in his arms. He'd present the bauble to her later. He had his heart's desire and she'd moaned his name and clung to him as her body bucked in ecstasy. His. All his.

When the mists between the worlds are thin...

She stretched and sighed as the magic flowed over her. Old black magic whispered into the night. Dark magic.

Not his magic.

Lucy's eyes fluttered open and her once clear expression clouded with potent need. She pressed her body against him and rubbed. Every inch of him jumped to answer, to push into the heat of her body and drown in the passion she offered all over again.

I call upon your power to arise and come to me...

Damian froze.

Lucy nuzzled his neck and ran her teeth along the sensitive skin. Her hands slid along his chest. "More," she whispered, her voice low.

Heart's desire called forth...

Spelled. She'd been spelled.

Like a bucket of ice water, dread splashed over him. Oh god, what had he done? She'd been spelled. The whole time. And he'd taken her, again and again. He was no better than one of those lurkers in clubs who took advantage of drunk women. What would happen when the spell wore off? When she found out what happened and realized what he did? He'd violated the one person his heart desired more than anything.

She already hated him. Now she'd despise him.

The soft look of love would disappear, replaced with loathing. And he'd mated with her. His griffin bond was for life and irreversible. He'd given her his heart, forever, and she didn't truly want it.

Prickling sensations ran up his neck and clutched his scalp in an icy grip. His gut twisted. The walls in the room closed in. He untangled himself from her limbs, her soft skin sliding along his. He sucked in a breath. He'd never feel this again. She'd never willingly touch him after the spell wore off, and she realized what he did.

He stood up.

Hippo was suspiciously silent, as if he, too, had no clue what to do.

Lucy rolled onto her side and looked up at him, her gaze warm and satiated, like melted honey. He could drown in the pools of her eyes.

"Hey," she said.

"Hey." He located his clothes and pulled them on.

Her eyebrows pinched in and she sat up. Her scent changed, gaining a tangy edge from worry. "What's wrong?"

Everything. He needed to get out of this room, away from his mate, away from the heat of her body and the fire in her gaze before he made a bad situation worse and caused more hurt. "I need to go."

"Now?"

"Yeah." He grabbed his sweater. The magical words whispered on the wind flowed over his body. An image of dark hair and darker eyes flashed through his memory. Her finger waggling wave. Her blowing kiss and jaunty walk.

Damian clutched the sweater in his hands and squeezed. He needed to find out who was responsible for the spell and he had a good idea where to start.

"It's two in the morning."

"Yeah." He raked a hand through his hair, like it would help tame it. "Police business."

"Oh." Her bottom lip jutted out.

He winced. He knew better than to lie to another shifter. Before he could stop himself, he leaned down and captured her mouth. He poured his heart into their last kiss. Told her all the things he wanted to say, all the things he admired about her, and how sorry he was. A goodbye to remember.

She melted into his arms. He'd never get the taste of her sweet tongue or feel of her smooth skin out of his memory.

He pulled away and stalked from the room without looking back. If he saw her desire, hurt, or confusion...if he saw her, he'd never leave.

Lucy pulled herself off the hard surface of the kitchen island and turned on the bright kitchen lights. A cool breeze brushed her bare skin, most likely a draft created from Damian's hasty retreat into the night only moments ago. Cold blood dampened any remaining heat thrumming in her veins.

He left.

Had this moment not meant as much to him as it did to her?

She scrambled to find her clothes and pull them on. The tattered remains of her undies went into the trash. The garbage bag crinkled, as if laughing at the symbolism. Her life was literally going down in the dumps.

Whispurr kept silent for the first time in her life and curled around Lucy's heart as if the gesture would somehow protect it from breaking.

Damian lied when he said he left for police business. Lied. To her face. His delectable scent turning rotten in the air. Even if she couldn't read body language and heartbeats, his phone was miles away when the sudden urge to flee overcame him.

Lucy brushed away the dampness on her cheeks. Stupid leaking eyes.

She should go home and sleep, but one look at the state of her kitchen and she knew that wasn't happening. Knowing her luck, some overly enthusiastic Health and Safety inspector would grant her a surprise visit tomorrow. The bin of dirty dishes shouldn't sit overnight anyway.

Her shoulders dropped and she dragged her heavy feet to the cleaning supplies. Time to disinfect and sanitize the kitchen. Time to remove all physical traces that this ever occurred.

She sniffed and started scrubbing. The fumes tingled her nose and left a bitter taste in her mouth, but her memory wouldn't forget Damian.

If only the heavy-duty kitchen spray worked on a broken heart.

Damian threw his keys on the kitchen counter and stomped to his laptop, his heavy footsteps echoing in the cold, large room. He hadn't closed his blinds before he left for work and the inky dark of the winter's night stared back at him.

He'd bonded to her.

If he closed his eyes, he'd feel her in his arms, hear her gasp in his ear and taste the sweetness of her skin. He glanced at the decorative box that sat on the nearby side table. Inside sat the first piece of his horde, the first item of value he ever owned. It was infused with his essence and intended for his mate.

For Lucy.

And now he'd never have a chance to give it to her.

Focus, Hippo hissed.

His griffin was right. He couldn't dwell on this right now. He needed to find out who was responsible and make them suffer.

He snarled as he loaded the surveillance footage. The video feed wasn't much good. He didn't dare install cameras inside the house. Who knew what he'd see. He wasn't a sick pervert or voyeur. The cameras showed a man entering Arabia's house, but none of the angles clearly showed his face. It wasn't the gray-haired businessman.

Damian loaded the audio next. The magic hit around nine last night. He fast forwarded.

There.

Arabia's voice whispered an incantation, barely audible over the static.

The hairs on his arms stood up.

Got her. He knew it. Now he'd make her...

Damian paused. What the hell did he do now? Smite her? He abhorred violence against women, and unless she physically attacked him, he wouldn't stoop to this option. She was also ravenborn. Even Damian knew better than to incur the wrath of the gods. He drummed his fingers along the top of his desk. Imprison her in a dark cave in a remote location?

Imprison.

His lips curled up.

He reached for his burner phone and punched in one of three numbers he knew by heart. He had a worse fate planned for Arabia. One that kept his hands clean, and avoided the divine retribution that went along with hurting the gods' favored messengers.

"Stillwater police department." A male officer answered the phone. Officer White judging from the nervous waver. Something must've unsettled him.

"Arabia Jensen cursed Stillwater with a malicious spell and caused the town-wide orgy." He didn't even know if the town-wide part was true, but if the spell hit him and Lucy, it probably ensnared a few other hapless victims as well. He prattled off Arabia's home address, kept his voice muffled and hung up once he finished. No response necessary. Let the court of public opinion condemn her.

CHAPTER EIGHT

WORK OF SHAME

Thursday, November 8th

Lucy slammed the register closed and offered a disheveled customer a tight smile. The morning clientele today was an unusual sort—half the customers appeared euphoric while the other half was a mix of stressed and depressed, hot messes. Lucy fell into the latter group.

The door chimed and Tanner walked in with a whoosh of cold air. Lucy did a double take. The glaring natural light streaming through the new storefront window allowed nothing to hide. Her employee's usually coifed hair was a little mussed, dark circles underlined bloodshot eyes and his shoulders slumped. His normal confidence and jaunty saunter had disappeared. Another member for Team Hot Mess.

"You're late," she grumbled without any heat.

Tanner grunted and grabbed his apron from behind the counter. "Sorry."

"Want to talk about it?" She slid a customer's drink across

the serving counter.

Tanner looked her up and down, taking in her hastily thrown together outfit—a questionably clean T-shirt and the jeans from yesterday. "Do you?"

"Nope."

"Me neither." He jerked his chin at the till, a silent way of telling her to get out of his station at the espresso machine. "Did you see Mrs. Bee's awning?"

How could she not? It was on the same street and the tattered remains of the yellow and black material hung from the warped metal frame. "Looks like someone tried to rip it off."

Tanner snorted. "Gossip around town is a lusty couple wanted to see if it would hold."

Lucy turned and gaped at him.

"Not me!"

She waited.

He shook his head.

"What else is gossip saying?" she asked and then held her breath. Did anyone know? Did anyone suspect? The customers were abnormally tight-lipped this morning, but Tanner had better sources. Her shower might've been short this morning, but she scrubbed her skin to remove any traces of Damian's potent scent. Even now, though, if she turned a certain way, she caught the manly musk of the griffin as if he's stamped his presence on her. Could other shifters detect it?

Tanner leaned down and whispered, "Someone cast a love spell."

"Seriously?"

"Arabia Jensen was arrested this morning."

She raised her eyebrows. "They think she cast a love spell?"

Tanner laughed. "Of course she did."

Lucy smiled and went back to wiping the counter. Arabia was friends with Kiera, but Lucy didn't really know the other woman. Not well, anyway. She never paid much attention to the gossip surrounding Arabia, either. That changed the moment she overheard two customers discussing over lattés how a hot cop allegedly took Arabia on a date. The hot cop was Damian. After that moment, Lucy started listening to the whispers about the raven shifter.

Arabia Jensen was a dynamic force of nature—too wild for Lucy, but she admired the raven shifter's directness and love for life. She couldn't find anything to hate about the other woman, and disliking someone for going on a date with a man she tried to hate seemed petty and pointless. Arabia and Damian's romance, whatever it had been, didn't last long anyway. If gossip was correct, the relationship started and ended with one date.

She'd be mad at Arabia for last night, but Lucy hadn't been spelled. How could she? Surely, she'd notice something like that. Unless the magic somehow granted her deepest, darkest fantasies come true. The gossip was wrong. Arabia probably did something else to get arrested.

She squeezed her eyes shut. Immediately, memories played with her mind. As if time rewound to make her relive the experience, she could taste him, feel him and see him. Damian's intense gaze, watching every reaction he wrought with each thrust and enjoying every minute of it. The strength of his arms, the wickedness of his tongue...

She snapped her eyes open. She couldn't daydream like this. She had work to do, and...and Damian left her.

She paused. Had he been spelled? Her stomach sunk. Was that why he ran off in such a hurry? Her mouth grew dry.

Whispurr tightened around her chest in a silent hug.

She glanced at the door, lungs in a knot.

She had only one way to find out why the night ended the way it did, but Damian was suspiciously absent. She wiped the wet rag along the counter. He hadn't been in all morning. Even

Mateo was notably missing-in-action. What the hell was going on? Lucy squeezed the rag. Water pooled on the counter and splattered her jeans.

Too much had transpired between Damian and her to disregard the experience or let it go without some sort of resolution. She'd find out what happened last night. She sighed and wiped up the pool of water.

If Damian thought he could wake her from a deep sleep with a spectacular sunrise and then take off, he was in for a big surprise.

CHAPTER NINE

A BRICK FOR YOUR THOUGHTS

Wednesday, November 21ˢᵗ

Lucy pulled her jacket hood close to her face to stave off the cold morning air as she walked to work. The echo of her footsteps against the sidewalk disrupted the quiet of the pre-rush hour. Not many people were up at this time. Definitely not a certain Stillwater detective.

Two weeks. Two whole weeks of Damian clearly avoiding her and the café. Once a daily patron more reliable than the tasty goodness of a snowshoe hare, she hadn't spotted his gem-cutting jawline or keen golden gaze since their night together. Occasionally, she'd catch his scent, but when she looked around, she was alone.

Her original determination to confront the griffin had waned, then dissipated with each passing day. Her ego could only take so much rejection, and clearly that's what Damian's avoidance was.

His shame-faced, sheepish partner still came in, always

looking on the verge of blurting apologies or information. Lucy refused to ask Mateo about Damian, and so far he'd maintained silence about his partner. Instead, he filled her in on his sister's latest adventures at college.

Lucy turned the corner and headed down the street toward the café. She used to anticipate Damian's visits, though she'd never admitted it until now.

Now.

She swallowed her bitterness. She had little to look forward to except long days full of forced smiles. Damian momentarily lifted her into a sublime light only to throw her back down into a pit of dullness. Ugh.

Lucy kicked an errant stone off the sidewalk. Wham, bam, thank you ma'am. Damian had ghosted on her.

Double ugh.

She needed to hunt. Maybe Laura or Kiera would come with her. Most of the time she went alone, being fiercely territorial and a solo hunter, but the company might help her forget.

Lucy stalked the final steps to the café's front door and froze.

Though the sun hadn't crested the horizon yet, her supernatural eyesight and the predawn light were enough for her to take in the scene that greeted her. Shattered pieces of the newly replaced window scattered along the sidewalk and in ugly neon orange spray paint, someone had written "Freak" across the entire store front.

Her shoulders sank. Just what she needed—another hike in her premium. And freak? Really? Not exactly original and not exactly the right audience. Almost everyone in Stillwater had some sort of supernatural ability.

This sleepy little town was a safe haven for people like her. That's what drew her to Stillwater. That's what drew everyone here.

She unlocked the door and mentally revised her morning list of chores. Take pictures, clean up glass, bake muffins, board window, scrub wall...

Lucy cursed. Why was someone targeting her business? This was her livelihood. She swung the door open and walked into the café. Glass crunched under her boots. A large red brick identical to the last one sat on a table near the window. An elastic band held a piece of paper to the brick. The cold November breeze from the gaping hole in her storefront teased the corners of the paper.

She took pictures before gently pulling the paper free by the corner. She should call the cops.

She squeezed her eyes shut. No. No more running to Damian for help. He'd ruthlessly find the culprit, she was sure of that, but he was already on the case. She didn't need to perform a damsel in distress act to get his attention.

Pinching the paper between her finger and thumb, she stomped to her office and found a sealable baggie to slide the paper into. There. If they needed prints, the evidence remained uncontaminated. Well, at least, not too contaminated.

She flattened the paper over her desk. A typed message read, "Leave."

Leave? That's it? No "or else" or some other ambiguous threat?

She opened the bag again and sniffed. A lingering scent teased her senses, but slipped away. She wasn't a bloodhound, her skills didn't rely on an exceptional sense of smell.

She resealed the bag and sat back. Window panes were expensive to replace and her insurance company would jack up their prices, if they hadn't already.

She drummed her fingers over the note on the desk.

After her father's brief appearance and hasty retreat from her life, she'd made a conscious decision to stay in Stillwater

70

and make it home. Some street-level thug and a one-night stand gone awkward weren't going to chase her from her territory. Nothing would keep her from what was hers.

She snarled and balled her hands into fists. Was this the work of her father?

The front door swished and the bell chimed. "Whoa. Lucy? You here?"

"Yeah, Tanner. In the back."

More glass crunched as Tanner made his way through the café. His perfectly gelled hair and handsome face poked through her office doorway. He'd rebounded quickly from whatever happened to him on the "Night of the Great Hex." His familiar scent filled her office. She now associated his soft cologne with comfort and safety. When had he changed from employee to family?

"You okay?" he asked.

She sighed and sank into her seat. "Just pissed."

"Have you called the cops?"

She flipped the letter over so Tanner couldn't read it and stood up. "Not yet. There's no emergency and I've taken pictures. They won't gain any new insight from this scene that they didn't glean from the last."

Tanner opened and closed his mouth. He repeated the motion a couple of times before speaking. "Lucy. This is a police matter. Don't be stupid."

"I'll call them later. I don't have time to deal with another interrogation." She crossed her arms. "And I'm not stupid."

His gaze narrowed. "No, you're not stupid. You know you should call this in."

She looked away.

"But you don't want to."

Her skin tingled.

"Does the reason you don't want to call have anything to do with the recent notable absence of a certain police detective?"

She turned to Tanner to find his knowing gaze watching her. She pursed her lips. "We have so much to do this morning. There's barely time to get this mess cleaned up before the morning rush starts and I can't afford to get pulled aside to answer the same questions all over again. The cops didn't find anything useful from the last broken window. I'm sure the vandal used gloves and covered his or her tracks just as well as they did the first time. I'll call it in, later, or mention it to Mateo when he arrives. Promise."

Tanner conducted a perfect eye roll and spun around. "I'll work on the spray paint."

"Have I told you you're awesome?" she called out after him.

"Not recently."

Gusts of cold air blew into the café with each patron entering and exiting. It was impossible to keep the area at a constant temperature. With the window boarded up, again, glimpses through the door were her only portal to the outside. Snow drifted down and a light dusting covered the steps to the courthouse across the street. Wet steps slapped against the soaked mat at the entrance and splattered muddy water against the tiles. Tanner and she took turns mopping up the mess.

Mateo walked in and approached the counter with a smile. "Hey, Luce. More window problems?"

"Unfortunately," she said, tone dry. "The regular for you?"

"And Damian." Mateo frowned, gaze calculating. His panther scent floated in the draft caused by the constant opening and closing of the door. "Unfortunately? I thought maybe there was an installation issue."

She punched in his order and Damian's and recited the total before it popped on the screen.

"Why didn't you call in this *unfortunate* event, Luce?"

Ugh. He used his papa Mateo I'm-going-to-scold-you voice

on her, the one Jewel loved to hate. Well, Lucy wasn't his little sister. She didn't have to put up with it.

"Figured the town was going through enough as is." Lucy shrugged.

Gossip had rolled into the café with reckless abandon. All sorts of salacious tales tumbled off the loose tongues of her recovering customers. Word in the café confirmed Arabia Jensen had been arrested for laying a monster of a love spell on the entire town.

Lucy still didn't believe the hype. She certainly hadn't been spelled. At least not by some random raven shifter. No, she'd fallen for Damian's considerable charms long before any third party hocus pocus. She'd fallen under Damian's spell that night, not Arabia's. Now, she desperately needed a self-respectable way to claw out of the pit he'd left her in.

Lucy pulled two takeaway cups from the stack and placed them beside the espresso machine. Usually she scribbled down the order in shorthand on the cups, but Tanner also knew the regulars and had already started the order.

Mateo waited for her to elaborate, his dark eyes flashing under the café's lights. At least that's what she assumed his stern, "I'm serious" expression meant.

She sighed. Maybe she loved to hate his protective older brother act as well. It wasn't his fault her windows were smashed or his partner was an arrogant jerk. "There wasn't much point in calling it in. Pretty much same MO as before."

"First, please stop using television police jargon." Mateo's gaze narrowed and his mouth compressed into a thin line. "And second, that's for us to decide."

Tanner shook his head. He thunked the metal frothing pitcher full of steamed milk on the counter. He turned to Lucy. "Exactly the same, except the spray paint and threatening letter."

Mateo and Lucy turned to the barista at the same time.

Lucy's mouth dropped open. How had he seen the letter? He must've spotted it when he popped into her office and snuck back later to have a look. Sly fox.

"Spray paint?" Mateo's dark eyebrows shot up. "I thought I smelled acetone."

Tanner had successfully cleaned off the spray paint in record time—faster and better than Lucy thought possible. Maybe Tanner was secretly a powerful warlock, slumming as a minimum-wage barista to gain life experience before he headed back to some evil lair to concoct a plan for world domination.

If he did, at least he'd spare her. At least she thought he would.

"I took pictures, and a piece of wood with spray paint on it chipped off when I was cleaning. I put it in a sealable bag in case you wanted a sample." Tanner poured the frothed milk into the takeaway cups. The smooth scent of heated milk and espresso curled around her.

"Great thinking, Tanner. I'll take the sample." He turned to Lucy. "And the note."

Lucy seriously considered firing Tanner. Or killing him. Sure, he was her friend and a damn good employee, but he shouldn't have told the truth. Family lied for each other, right?

Whispurr snorted.

Both men stared at her and waited.

Her shoulders dropped. "In my office, also in a sealed baggie. I only touched one of the corners to pull it from the brick."

"Pull it from..." Mateo pinched the bridge of his nose. "This is escalating Lucy. A threat is more serious than a broken window. Show me the letter. Please."

Five minutes after Mateo left the café, quiet and unimpressed with Lucy, Damian stormed through the front entrance. The bell chimed with an unneeded warning. Damian stalked to the counter. His ordinary sweater and jeans did little to hide his extraordinary body. His wet boots hit the tiles with deadly accuracy.

Lucy stood still.

Energy swirled around Damian, violent and potent. The air sucked from the room, leaving a muscular ball of barely contained rage as the centerpiece. The lights flickered. One word. One wrong move and he'd unleash the menacing power.

"Whoa," Tanner said, muscles tense.

Lucy agreed.

So did the customers, who pulled back and jumped out of the way as if a freight train barreled toward them instead of a Stillwater detective.

Mateo must've told him about the window the second he left the coffee shop. Traitor.

She wiped her hands on her pants and tugged her shirt down. *Breathe. Just breathe.*

I can't decide whether we should claw his pretty face or jump him, Whispurr mused.

"Lucy," Damian growled through clenched teeth.

"Damian." She lifted her chin. He couldn't intimidate her. No way would she let him know how much he hurt her by leaving. She had nothing else to hide, and certainly nothing to be ashamed of. Well, except for contaminating evidence and not calling in the vandalism.

After Mateo got through scolding her, she had to admit it was a pretty dumb move. Aside from not wanting to take the time to properly deal with the vandalism this morning, she didn't want to acknowledge it happened. One brick could've been explained away as the actions of a troubled youth with too much time and no personal ill-will directed at her or her business. Twice, though...Twice meant she was being specifically targeted, and she couldn't ignore it. Reporting it meant accepting this happened and gave the current feeling of unease gnawing at her gut validation and more power than she'd like.

"Why didn't you call it in?" He dropped his voice.

Like rats scrambling from a sinking ship, everyone in the café bottlenecked to escape through the front door.

Tanner followed close behind. "I'm taking my break," he called over his shoulder.

Lucy narrowed her eyes. Deserter.

"Lucy," Damian snarled.

The front door shut, leaving them alone. His lion and eagle scent coiled around her with a magical punch, like some sort of hypnotic embrace. Why did he have to smell so good? Why did he look so good when he was furious?

"Why did you leave?" She snapped her mouth shut. Dammit. So much for playing it cool. What happened to her confident and tactful plan?

Damian's head jerked back. "Why did I—"

"Leave. It was a dick move." Pun not intended.

Tension remained in his posture, but he tamed the potent griffin energy, pulling it in so she no longer choked on the power.

"I thought..." He looked away.

He thought what? Why didn't he finish the thought? Why was he clenching his jaw so hard?

He needed to speak, dammit.

Why wasn't he speaking? Had she actually shocked the big bad griffin into silence? Fine. She had plenty to say to fill the silence. "You thought what? That all women like to be left naked on a kitchen counter and avoided afterward?" She rubbed her arms.

The creases between his eyes smoothed out. His gaze softened. "I thought you'd hate me."

Her blood boiled. "Oh, I hate you."

His mouth flattened.

"I hate you for leaving."

He curled his hands into giant fists. The floorboards creaked. His griffin energy snapped around him again. He must really be on edge to reveal his power. She'd never seen him display the griffin essence so visibly before, if ever. He normally kept it completely controlled to hide his true nature. Most people wouldn't figure it out, though, even if they were around to see it. To most, griffins were still mythological beasts. Any spectators would assume the crackling in the air was a demonstration of Damian's warlock abilities.

Lucy saw it. She felt it. Hell, she could taste it. His power appeared clearer than it ever had before, as if she was somehow more attuned to it now. Damian stood like some sort of sexy Van de Graaff generator, his power streaking out from his body in bolts of blue, gold and white lightning. The griffin energy called to her, pulling her forward. She bucked under the potency and looked away.

"You should've called it in, Luce," he said, his tone low and rumbling, yet...tender?

She looked up.

The anger no longer flashed in his gaze, the tension eased from his shoulders. Whatever Damian learned from her response to his magic softened his demeanor.

"Well, I didn't want to ruin your impressive effort to avoid me," she muttered. Why had he thought she'd hate him *before* he left? She frantically tried to make sense of his words, ping-ponging information around her brain like a crazed game of table tennis.

A slow smile spread across his face. Slow and knowing. Salacious. Memories of their time together flashed through her mind.

Lucy straightened, the shift in Damian's attitude surprising. And intoxicating.

"Oh, trust me," he said. "I'll correct that error as soon as possible."

"But?" her heart hammered. What did he mean? Why was he acting so protective when he obviously wanted nothing to do with her? Was this some sort of weird griffin thing? Once conquered, she was forgotten and cast to the side, forever branded as his but just another token piece in his empire? Ugh. Griffins.

"But nothing." His grin turned cruel. "In the meantime, I'll find out who broke your window and make them regret it."

CHAPTER TEN

BEAST FRIENDS FOR NEVER

Monday, November 26th

Damian's skin chaffed with each minute he sat in the SUV on yet another stakeout. People thought police work was glamorous or lively and spent heroically chasing thugs through dimly lit alleys. In reality, he spent most of his time sitting on his ass. Streetlights and the soft glow from the surrounding buildings illuminated the dark interior. He wanted to rip these civilian clothes off and hunt in the forest or find the vandal harassing Lucy's café and exact the cost of the window from his or her hide, not sit in awkward silence with his partner. Granted, the silence was his fault, as was the vein threatening to burst from Mateo's forehead.

Just shut up for once and wait, Hippo drawled. *You dropped a doozy on him.*

The smell of stale coffee and paper filled the cabin of the vehicle along with their scents. The presence of another big cat often set his griffin on edge—the lion part of his dual nature needing to dominate and set the other feline in their place—but he always relaxed around Mateo.

"What the fuck were you thinking?"

Damian jumped in his seat and turned to his partner. The leather seat creaked. After Damian confessed his involvement with the case, Mateo had fumed without speaking to him for the last thirty minutes.

"I can't believe you illegally installed police-issue surveillance equipment in Arabia Jensen's home. You're a better cop than that," Mateo said.

"I wasn't thinking. Were you thinking when you decided to see if Mrs. Bee's awning would survive a session of hide the sausage with Kiera?" Mateo's earlier confession in the night had spurred Damian to make one of his own. Now he regretted telling his partner about his involvement in the Jensen case. He'd meant to make Mateo feel better, but his decision completely backfired.

"We were under magical influence at the time..." Mateo glared at him. If looks could kill, Damian wouldn't leave this vehicle alive. "It's not the same and you know it."

"I thought Arabia was up to something and wanted to protect..." He looked out the side window.

His griffin screeched. *Protect what is ours.*

Damian winced at the piercing sound staving his brain.

"Lucy," Mateo finished for him. He ran a hand down his face. If his partner understood anything of Damian's motives, it was the need to protect a loved one. "It won't hold up in court, you know."

"I know," he grumbled. "That's why I called it in anonymously."

"You could lose your job."

"I know." He'd already said he wasn't thinking. He wanted to make Arabia pay.

"I could lose mine."

His gut twisted. "No. You didn't know until now."

"The judge is a fucking sphynx," Mateo said.

Hippo snorted, obviously unimpressed.

"She'll pick up on a lie," Mateo said.

Damian shrugged. "During your investigation, you were unaware of the identity of the informant. There are ways around the truth."

"I could still get burned by your blunder."

His stomach sunk lower. He never intended for his partner to get hurt by this. He shouldn't have told Mateo. Sometimes ignorance wasn't just bliss, it was plausible deniability. "I'll throw myself on my sword if it comes to that, but I highly doubt the prosecutors or the defense lawyer will ask you for my identity. As far as they're concerned, the caller was anonymous. They never ask questions they don't already know the answer to and only three people, including myself, know the truth."

Mateo raked a hand through his hair and cursed. "Who else fucking knows?"

"White."

"You told that idiot?"

Damian winced. "I logged out the equipment and he followed up on it. He's not actually an idiot. He figured it out on his own."

Silence descended in the vehicle again. Mateo's mouth still twisted in a snarl, but the tension had left his shoulders.

"Someone's already been asking a lot of questions," Mateo said after a while.

"Chase Baron." Damian grunted. He knew all about the hotshot lawyer from LA who currently defended Arabia against the seventeen felony counts of magical coercion, and possession and felony misuse of a divine essence. Not only did he have an excellent track record, but he was a werewolf alpha.

"Yeah."

"Fuck him."

Mateo turned to him "You illegally installed surveillance technology in and around his lover's home and set up Arabia for some serious jail time. I'm sure he'll have stronger words for you when he finds out."

"*If* he finds out." Damian scowled. "And his ill-behaved raven cast a spell that..." He curled his hands into fists. If he hadn't destroyed the recordings, he could've learned more about the spell Arabia used. Reduced the background interference, slowed it down, and extracted the exact words. Instead, he'd disposed of any trace the recordings existed on his home laptop and used technology and magic to wipe the equipment. White had destroyed the logs. The Sphynx might discern a lie from truth, but the court system still required physical evidence for an actual conviction.

He needed to retrieve the surveillance equipment from Arabia's home, but as an active crime scene, he planned to avoid the cabin until the pandemonium had lessened. He couldn't risk contaminating the scene right now for something as insignificant as a few bugs no one else was looking for. One of the biggest mistakes criminals made was returning to the scene. Only an emergency would drag him back to that place.

Was he a criminal? Damian snorted. No. He was a good griffin. Most of the time. He only lost his temper when someone threatened what was his. Arabia had done exactly that.

Mateo glanced over at him again.

"What the actual fuck was that spell?"

Mateo shrugged.

"Find out!"

Mateo tensed and turned his shoulders toward him. "You're not the only one with problems, you know. Find out your goddamn self."

Damian straightened.

"I'm not your minion, and this isn't your kingdom, *Griffin*. You get that, right?"

Fuck. He'd managed to piss off one of his only friends. His chest tightened. "I'm an asshole."

"You're just now figuring that out?"

Damian slumped in his seat, his clothes whispering against the leather. "Yeah."

Mateo's glare softened. "Is it so bad it's irretrievable?"

"I bonded to her." He spoke to the dash, and silence answered him.

Mateo sucked in a breath. "Isn't that…"

"Yeah." Forever. Irreversible.

Mateo reached over and man-clamped his shoulder. "It will work out. I'm sure Lucy doesn't hate you."

"Oh, she hates me, but not for the reason I thought."

Mateo barked out a laugh. "Isn't that always the way with women?"

Damian snorted.

Another bout of silence followed, but this time, more companionable.

Mateo drummed his fingers on the steering wheel. "Have you tried apologizing?"

"Of course, I've—" Damian paused. His mind scrambled. Had he? He told her he'd fix his mistake but had he properly apologized? "Well, shit."

Mateo smirked. "You're not exactly great at saying sorry."

Damian's skin prickled. The words stuck to the inside of his throat. He grunted and turned to his partner. "I'm sorry I'm such an asshole and a bad partner. I shouldn't have put you in this position."

Mateo grumbled. After a tense minute, he nodded. "That wasn't half bad for an apology. If you need more practice, I have a few other complaints."

"Don't push it."

"Like you don't deserve it."

"Fair enough."

Mateo settled back in his seat. "What's your plan?"

"I need to find out the exact spell."

"Does it matter? You need to fix things with Lucy, regardless."

His partner had a point. Maybe he should go home, grab his mating bauble and confess his feelings and deepest desires. He paused and mulled the idea over. No. Too much. She might balk. He needed to show her he was worthy first. He needed to be armed with information and a list of accomplishments.

He ran a hand through his hair. Where the hell did he start?

CHAPTER ELEVEN

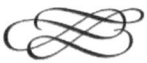

CAN'T HANDLE THE VANDAL

Tuesday, December 4th

Lucy held her breath and pushed the coffee cup across the counter toward Damian. His smile grew, nearly blinding her with his white teeth. The familiar dual scent coiled around her and his griffin power reached out and licked her skin. She shivered and ignored the ache his magical touch ignited.

Her lynx purred.

In the last couple of weeks, Damian had removed all pretense from his actions. The mighty griffin hit on her. All the time. As though he threw caution out the door and turned the deadbolt, he focused his considerable charms on her.

The effect was devastating.

Every time she stood on the precipice of giving in and falling for him, she remembered how he left her naked on her kitchen counter.

Yup. That did it.

"Did you hear someone bought the office building on the

corner?" He ignored the coffee cup and waited for her response.

"Oh?" Resist. Resist. "Who?" Dammit.

Damian shrugged, but flashed his pretty teeth. "No one knows."

"Aren't you some hotshot detective? Couldn't you find out?"

"I could, but I'm trying this new thing called *behaving*."

She almost laughed at his scowl. Almost. "How's that going for you?"

"Torture." He leaned forward. His wool sweater accentuated his broad shoulders and his dark hair shone under the lights.

She gripped the hard countertop to stop her traitorous hands from reaching out to run along his chest or tease her fingers through his silky soft hair.

"Can I give you a lift home after work tonight?" he asked, glancing out the window. The sun had set hours ago.

"No, you may not."

His griffin energy crackled against her skin like a sparkler. "Have you been to our forest for a run recently?"

Our forest. Interesting. When he'd referred to it in the past, it was either "the forest" or completely his. Now, all of a sudden, the majestic griffin wanted to share.

"Of course not," she lied. She'd gone on a run every night since Damian had left her. It helped take off the edge from the bitterness and hurt. And aching need. He'd lit a fire in her and now she scrambled to put it out.

He straightened. "I swear I saw your tracks."

He would've sensed her lie, too. She shrugged and turned to the counter. No one occupied the shop but them. Tanner was gone. The café became suspiciously quiet when Damian visited, and her employee pulled a disappearing act. She needed to talk to Tanner about that.

"Are you making my customers leave?" She turned back to the griffin.

He winked.

"That's not an answer." Her hands flew to her hips. "You know it's wrong, right? You can't send people away willy-nilly."

"I'm being good." He held his hands out wide.

Oh, he was good all right. Good in bed and good at lying. Ugh. "That's not the word I'd use to describe you."

His expression shuttered. "I know."

For weeks, shiny jewelry and flowers kept turning up on her doorstep without a card. Damian didn't need to leave one. His delicious scent wrapped around the gifts and let her know immediately who sent them. He offered her a ride home after work almost every night and asked her out for runs. Why? He said leaving her had been an error he meant to correct, but despite all his efforts to win her over, the stubborn griffin hadn't apologized for leaving her alone, naked and vulnerable. Was he trying to mend a friendship or rekindle the passion between them or something else entirely? "Damian, why are you here?"

"Besides the coffee?"

"Yes, besides your addiction to caffeine." Most people asked for decaf this late into the night, but not Detective Charming.

Damian paused, probably to mull over possible responses. If the old Damian were here, he'd say something jarring or make a joke out of the situation. Would he revert back to his previous ways, or was this new, more alluring Damian sticking around—the man she always caught a glimpse of under the cold façade. Which one was real? Which one was the true Damian? Both? Neither?

"I want to give you new words to describe me," he said.

"New words?"

"Better words." He picked up his coffee, gave her a silent salute and turned to leave.

Lucy sank against the counter. New words? She already had an arsenal of words to describe Detective Damian Charming. They either fell in the bad column or the good one. As if his very nature of two combined animals gave him a split personality, she couldn't decide which persona was the real Damian, and which one she liked best. Or the least. And did it even matter? Despite all the bad, her heart ached for him. All of him. Still.

If she couldn't find a way to keep hating him, she'd end up hating herself.

Damian looked over his shoulder at her and stopped. He turned and frowned, gaze raking her body. He stepped forward and hesitated. His gaze turned soft and he opened his mouth.

Something small and dark smashed through the window. The glass shattered, spraying shards of gem-size debris all over the café. The glass clinked against the table tops and spilled to the floor with in a tinkling cascade.

Damian barreled into her. The air whooshed from her lungs. Her back slammed against the floor and Damian's muscled body landed on top of her. They slid to a stop, slightly past the counter, giving Lucy a clear view of her destroyed window.

"Not again!" she wailed.

"Stay down."

Lucy turned to Damian, his gaze wild. He'd shielded her from the danger with his body, and now he pinned her to the floor in a position reminiscent of their night together. Images of him on top of her with the kitchen lights dancing along his muscles, his tattoo across his chest coming to life as he moved above her. Warmth flushed her cheeks. Heat pooled between her legs. A familiar ache returned.

Damian's nose flared. His razor focus softened. He licked

his lips and leaned down. He was going to kiss her, and damn her traitorous body, she was going to let him.

Before his lips reached hers, he stopped. Visibly shaking himself, he looked away toward the broken window. "Another brick."

Before her body could betray her any more than it already had, Damian swiftly stood up and brought her with him. The lights spun and a wave of dizziness passed over her from the quick transition. Damian gripped her arms and steadied her. When she stopped swaying, he let her go.

"Are you okay?" His gaze raked her body again, looking for damage.

"I'm good."

"Stay here." He sprinted. Leaving a wake of cold air in his path.

Lucy had never seen him move so fast, but it was a thing to behold. Damian sprinted to the door, flung it open and disappeared into the night.

Stay here? Whispurr snorted.

Lucy laughed. *Like I'd miss this.*

She ran after him. Pulling on her lynx senses, the cold December air burned her nose as she followed Damian's trail. She didn't make it far. Damian had slipped into the back alley and stood in the loading area next to a dumpster. Dark energy lingered on the bricks of the building and the pavement.

Damian vibrated. He held his clenched hands out to the side and his face up to the moon.

He'd lost the trail. The vandal had escaped. If his protective instinct hadn't kicked in, he wouldn't have dove on top of her and wasted time. He could've caught the asshole targeting her business.

Really? You're angry he wanted to protect you? Whispurr poked her brain.

No, she wasn't. Her skin tingled. She was the opposite of

angry. Damian had lost his chance to catch the bad guy and now he fought for control. Lucy didn't know much about griffins. Heck, she hadn't known they existed until she met Damian. She'd seen him shift before, but she'd never worked up the courage to ask how much the technical aspects varied from her own transformations. The strain on Damian's face and the tension in his body resembled that of a shifter fighting for control with their inner beast. His griffin wanted out and Damian did his best to stop that from happening.

Lucy placed a hand on his arm. His magic tingled against her skin. This was the first time she'd voluntarily touched him since their night together, and in response, griffin energy reached out and wrapped around her in an invisible hug.

"Stay with me," she whispered.

Damian vibrated. His magic pulsed.

"Don't shift. The guy is long gone."

Damian turned away from the moon and focused on her hand. His brow furrowed. He took long, deep breaths and stared at her hand as if it provided an anchor to reality. Maybe it did.

"You won't catch him now, and you can't expose your nature to whomever might be watching." This was an alley not a deserted forest. For whatever reason, Damian had kept his true identity hidden from the residents of Stillwater. She didn't want him to throw that all away now. Not for her. "It's not worth it."

"Don't you get it, Luce?" He finally looked at her, his gaze fiery thunderbolts.

She shook her head, not trusting her voice. What was there to get?

"You're worth everything." He turned and gripped her head with both hands. His mouth crashed down on hers and stole her breath away. Her knees grew weak and she clung to him. Desperate and full of need, his kiss liquefied her bones.

Putty in his hands, he could mold her into anything, play with her unhindered, and not only would she let him, she'd beg for more.

Before she lost all sense of reality, Damian drew away, regret tugging at his features. "Let me drive you home."

Home? Why the hell would she want to go home right now? A few minutes longer and she would beg him to have his way with her against a grungy dumpster.

She straightened, demanding her limbs to cooperate and met Damian's gaze. How could she stand on her own after that kiss? Conflict warred on his face—need, longing and fear.

Fear? That couldn't be right. What on earth would scare the mighty griffin?

You, Whispurr said.

Me? I couldn't harm him. Nor would she want to.

No, you idiot. He's scared for you. Someone attacked your business again while you were inside.

Understanding gnawed at her brainwaves. He wanted to get her home where she'd be safe. His words might've been a request, but his tone and expression pleaded with her not to argue. Damian's savior complex had kicked in full force.

"Okay. Let me get my things."

After they stopped at the café to pick up her stuff and board the window—she conveniently hadn't put the last board away yet—Damian packed her into his SUV and drove her home. They hardly said two words to each other the entire time.

She didn't know exactly what went through Damian's head, but she could guess. Part of him wanted to shift and chase down the person who threatened her, and the other part wanted to get her home safely.

All of Lucy wanted to revisit the bone-melting kiss in the alley. No amount of remembering the naked and alone feeling on the kitchen counter could drive away her need to taste him. Her lips still tingled from his mouth.

Damian pulled onto her street and headed for her house. His grip tight on the steering wheel, his gaze focused on the road.

Maybe it was a good thing he stopped the kiss when he did. Her body might burn up with need, but he still hadn't apologized. Jumping him now would only add to their issues.

When she finally stood at her front door, she turned to Damian and waited.

His lips pressed together in a firm line. "Lock your door."

"Why?" She folded her arms. "They'll just go through the window."

"Lucy, I'm serious."

Wow. Apparently, Mateo wasn't the only one capable of the parental lecture voice. "So am I. At the rate this is going, I'd rather they come through the door. Do you have any idea how my premium will skyrocket after this?"

Understanding flashed through his gaze. "Let me take care of it."

"My premium?"

"The window," he ground out.

"No."

His body tensed. "No?"

"I can take care of myself, Charming."

Damian stepped up onto the landing with her. She froze. He leaned down and ran his hand down her cheek. His skin and magic burned as if his simple touch branded her.

"I'm not your responsibility." Her voice sounded weak to her own ears. Dammit. She wasn't weak.

Whispurr snorted. *You are weak. In the knees.*

Shut up.

Make me.

"Yet," he said.

"What?" Hang on. What had she said last? Her brain scrambled to pick up the lost conversation—*thanks,*

Whispurr—but Damian shook his head and stepped back.

"Goodnight, Lucy."

"Uh..."

Before she could figure out a proper response, he jogged down the steps and climbed into his vehicle. She stood, numb and cold, and watched him drive away until the SUV slipped into the inky darkness of the night.

CHAPTER TWELVE

INN ONE DAY, OUT THE NEXT

Wednesday, December 5th

Damian tossed the bag onto the floor in front of the passenger side and slid into the driver's seat. The air rushed into the vehicle with him, bringing the scent of evergreens and impending snow. He started the SUV and headed toward Lucy's home. The tires crunched along the gravel leading out of the forest. Rays of sunlight shot through breaks in the canopy and danced along his windshield.

A dark essence had coated the bricks of the surrounding buildings in the alley last night after he lost the vandal. Whomever had thrown the brick possessed powerful magic, strong enough to leave a slimy residue. Even if he had shifted to a griffin, he wouldn't have caught that asshole when they had such a head start. Lucy was right to stop him.

The anger simmering in his veins settled at the thought of his lynx and the kiss in the dark alley. Maybe he could fix this. He was certainly trying.

In the meantime, he'd hunt down the culprit and make the person pay for damaging Lucy's property. Hell, with the rage vibrating through his body, the criminal would be lucky to make it to booking alive. Damian squeezed the steering wheel. He had White looking into visitors from out of town who arrived on or before the first act of vandalism. It would take time, though. Without a warrant, the local hotels didn't need to comply with requests and often didn't—valuing their customers' privacy. White would have to dig deep to make a list.

Something Mateo said the other night nagged him. The lawyer Chase Baron. He mentioned Chase was Arabia's lover. When had that happened? Acting as Arabia's counsel for a month hardly gave him the time or opportunity to start a romantic relationship. At least not the kind Mateo hinted at. When exactly did the lawyer get in town?

Damian drummed his fingers along the cold steering wheel. His breath puffed out in little clouds in the cool morning air.

The surveillance feed from Arabia's house on the night of the great hex showed a man entering the raven shifter's home. The face was never clear in any of the shots, but the height and build fit. Chase could've been Arabia's lover that night, and the target of her spell. But why was he in town?

If he came to see Arabia, surely she didn't need a spell to secure him. What if he came to Stillwater for another reason? Something more nefarious?

Damian pulled the SUV over and eyed the street leading to Lucy's. He dug out his phone from his pocket.

Mateo picked up on the second ring. "Savage."

"What do you know about Chase Baron?"

"Hello to you, too, dickwad."

Damian grunted. Obviously, the surveillance thing still pissed off his partner.

"Wait. Chase Baron? As in Jensen's lawyer?"

"Yeah. I think he arrived in Stillwater before the spell."

"And?"

"And the recent vandalism doesn't fit a local."

"You think that fancy lawyer from LA threw a brick through your mate's window? Why the fuck would he do that?"

Damian growled. "It doesn't really fit, I know, but I need to eliminate him as a suspect."

"What about that silver-haired guy you saw in town?"

"Officer White is looking into him for me, and all other newcomers. Once we have a name, we'll dig deeper. Right now, I want to check out Baron."

"He's staying at the Two Swan's Inn."

"I'll head there now. Want to meet me?" Well, he'd go to the inn after he stopped by Lucy's to drop off the bag at her doorstep.

"No." A pause. "Just..."

"What?"

"Don't go as yourself."

Damian gripped the steering wheel. The leather squeaked. "The owner knows me. His dogs like me. Why should I bother with glamour?"

"Exactly. Grant knows you and might tell Baron who stopped by to ask questions. You can't poke around Chase Baron and not expect him to poke back. The last thing we need is for him to figure out your role in this debacle."

"No poking the bear. Got it." Mateo hooked up with the bear shifter, Kiera, so if anyone was poking the bear... Damian swallowed the laughter bubbling up from his chest. If Mateo wasn't pissed at him anymore, he'd tell him to fuck off or make some sort of comment about the irony.

Silence.

All right then. Still angry. Still pining for his bear-shifter lady-love. "You okay?"

"Yeah. I might head over to the Clover Club later."

Damian checked his watch. Well, it was five in the afternoon somewhere. "Alone?"

His partner growled at him and hung up. Guess that was a yes.

Sunlight flickered and danced through breaks in the surrounding evergreen forest as Damian navigated the SUV along the winding road. He clutched the steering wheel in a death grip and glared at the chunky silver rings on his fingers. One ring camouflaged his griffin essence twenty-four-seven so he could work amongst the other supernatural beings of Stillwater undetected—his kind had been mercilessly hunted by demons and other vicious entities and he had no wish to announce his presence in Stillwater. The other ring, once activated, obscured his appearance and property. Although he looked like himself, no one would recognize him or recall any identifying details.

Damian wove his griffin essence around the glamour ring and magically flicked the on switch. Mateo might be pissed at him, but his partner still had his back. Neither of them could afford Baron's scrutiny.

His phone rang from where it sat on the passenger seat. He pulled over and hit the accept button without reading the screen. "Charming."

"I told you to leave the window for me to deal with." Lucy hissed.

Damian smiled and threw the gear shift into park. He relaxed into his seat. "Yes, you did."

And he tried to respect her wishes on the matter, he really did. But he failed. Terribly. He had money to spare and the connections to get the window replaced faster than any insurance company.

"You can pay me back," he said, not meaning a word.

"I thought you were trying to behave."

"I never said I was any good at it."

Lucy sputtered—an adorable sound between a laugh and a groan. "Stay out of my business, *Charming*."

"No."

She growled and hung up.

Damian smiled at his phone before stuffing it into his pocket. Time to visit the inn. He maneuvered the vehicle down the last stretch of road and pulled up to the Two Swans Inn. The expansive log cabin sprawled over a cleared section amongst the surrounding Stillwater forest. The soft golden glow of lights welcomed guests to enter.

Grant Ward stepped from the entrance and approached the vehicle. Graying with a wiry build, the inn's owner held himself with the confidence of a man who lived his life with few regrets. Grant also had a sharp eye. Luckily, Damian's charm also included his SUV and licence plate.

Two large German Shepherds bounded out of the inn after their owner, spraying gravel everywhere. Rocks pelted the side of his vehicle. Bonnie and Clyde. Sweet as syrup when they liked you, mean as hell when they didn't.

"Settle." Grant ran a hand down the back of Bonnie's large head. The dogs sat, but remained tense. Their ears pinged forward as they watched Damian.

Damian slipped from the car and shut the door, his muscles stiff from chasing down rabbits to leave on Lucy's doorstep. He hunted larger game, and those little fuckers could move. He pulled on a heavy winter jacket.

"Hi, I'm Grant Ward, the owner of Two Swans." Grant held his hand out. "Wasn't expecting any visitors today. We're fully booked. How can I help you?"

Damian smiled and shook the man's hand, his skin tough and calloused. He smelled like feathers, pond water and dog hair. At least Damian's glamour spell worked. Grant would've recognized him right away, otherwise. "I'm here to see Chase."

"He's out." Grant rubbed the short stubble on his jaw. "And who are you?"

"Oh, sorry. That's rude of me. My name is John. I'm an old friend of Chase's from grade school."

"You don't look like a John."

Damian sighed and let his exhaustion pull at his limbs. "You're not the first person to tell me that. In fact, Chase said something similar to me years ago."

Grant narrowed his eyes.

Dammit. The old man didn't buy it. "I can't believe he's been here over a month and I just found out."

Grant's expression relaxed a little. "Well, now. He came the day the spell hit. With all the hoopla happening afterward, he was probably too busy to call an *old friend*."

Damian nodded and mentally crossed Chase off the suspect list. He'd arrived in town after at least two of the incidences. They'd have to focus on other newcomers to Stillwater. "I was really looking forward to catching up with him. We lost touch after we moved, and I don't have his contact information. I'll drive back to town and see if I can catch him there."

Grant folded his arms.

"Thanks again for your help."

"Sure." Grant unfolded his arms to shake the hand Damian offered. Polite and respectful, the innkeeper didn't trust him. Instead, he watched the SUV drive away from the inn until Damian finally turned the corner. He pulled out his phone from his pocket and hit Mateo's contact information.

"What now?" his partner growled.

"I'm going to be out of town for a bit. Cover for me." He hung up and tossed the phone on the passenger seat. His partner would have a lot of questions Damian couldn't answer.

Lucy had trusted him with personal information years ago, and he kept his promise. He wasn't about to break it now.

CHAPTER THIRTEEN

DADDY DEAREST

Damian pulled up to the dilapidated single-wide trailer. The white and faded teal paint covering the metal siding of the late '60s model was chipped and peeling. Someone had attached tires to the roof for insulation, but took little care with installing them properly. It looked as though they just tossed them up there, wiped their hands and said, "That'll do."

The home sat on a small plot in a trailer park for humans, about a five hour drive north from Stillwater. He'd driven the rest of the day and into the night to get here. Maybe he should check into a hotel and visit in the morning.

Let's get this over with, Hippo said.

Always the voice of reason. He'd crash somewhere later and head back to Stillwater tomorrow after he rested.

He stepped from the SUV, shut the door, and triggered the alarm. This wasn't the only defunct residence in the park and he'd passed more than one unsavory character on his way in.

With a deep breath, he walked up the temporary grate steps and avoided touching the warped and rusted railing that smelled of blood, booze and grime. The metal groaned with each step. He yanked the screen door open and nearly went over the side of the railing. The door came off the hinges and dangled from his hand. He stared at the door, covered in flaking white paint, and the ripped wire mesh screen. What the hell? Was this some sort of gag door? He looked around. No one nearby.

He threw the tin-like screen door over the railing. It hit the dirt packed ground with a clatter. The broken screen poked up in the air like a flag.

Damian turned back to the trailer and rapped his knuckles on the door.

"Wahhhyuwaaaaa?" A garbed bellow hollered from inside.

Damian shrugged, turned the door handle and stepped inside. The stagnant air reeked of mold, mildew, smoke, booze and lynx. The windows were lined with tinfoil, and garbage littered the counters and floor. A threadbare rug matted the living room, showing the worn path to the sunken couch from the door, and the walls leaked a brown liquid from habitual chain smoking and lack of ventilation.

A man sprawled on the couch. Long and lean, he would've been huge in his prime, but age and mistreatment had left him scrawny. His pale skin stretched over bones and his dirty white tank top sagged over his chest. Grease lined his jeans and caked on his skin and under his nails.

Damian had kept tabs on the man over the years and the reports said he found odd-jobs, including working on engines to support his drinking habit.

Earl May sat up, raked his greasy hair from his face and blinked at Damian with the same honey-colored gaze as Lucy's. Same, but different. Lucy's eyes shone with wit and vitality; his had lost their luster a long time ago.

"You!" Earl threw a beer bottle at him

Damian ducked. The glass bottle flew through the air and crashed against the wall. Cheap beer sprayed everywhere.

"Hello, Earl." Damian stepped into the mobile home and let the door slam shut behind him. His dark shadow fell over Lucy's dad.

"What do you want?" Earl sneered at him and eyed his spilled beer as though he considered licking it up.

"Where've you been these last few weeks?"

"None of yer fucking business." Earl rocked forward to stand.

Damian moved closer. One excuse. He needed one excuse to wipe this foul shifter's presence from this earth.

Earl's gaze darted around the mobile. He licked his lips and sat back onto the couch, fingers twitching and knee bobbing up and down. "I've been here."

"The whole time?"

Earl scowled. "I've made a few trips to town for work."

"You've stayed out of Stillwater?"

Earl leaned to the side and spat into a can. He missed, and the beer stained spit hit the side of the metal container and dribbled down to the carpet. Earl grumbled then shrugged. He turned back to Damian. "You made it clear, *Detective*, what would happen if I attempted to contact my daughter again or returned to town."

Damian crossed his arms.

Earl flashed his jagged teeth at him—his smile menacing, stained from chronic smoking, and missing a number of teeth.

"You could've just called." Earl sneered. "I'm so honored by yer presence."

Just kill him, Hippo growled.

I promised Lucy.

"I wanted to see the truth for myself," he said. Shifters lied too easily over the phone and he couldn't read any of the sensory information from a distance. If Earl was involved, a phone call would also tip off the lynx shifter and make it more difficult for Damian to track him down later.

103

"Have you finally come to kill me?" Earl asked.

Even he knows he deserves it, Hippo said.

"Do I have a reason to?" Damian asked.

Earl's fake smile turned cruel. "Do you need a reason? I see murder in yer eyes."

Damian scowled. "The only reason you're alive right now is your daughter begged me to spare your life."

"Is that so?" A calculating look flashed across Earl's gaze.

"If you ever come near her that will change."

The calculation fled from his expression. Whatever he saw in Damian's face told the man he wasn't joking or making idle threats.

Earl nodded and with one last murderous glare, Damian left the trailer. He couldn't wipe Earl from the face of this earth, yet, but he could scrub his skin clean from the stink of Earl's home and the taint of standing in the same room with him. Damian jumped in his SUV and headed for the nearest hotel with a clean shower.

CHAPTER FOURTEEN

THE SASSY LIBRARIAN

Morning, Friday, December 7th

Damian's footsteps echoed against the concrete slab floor as he made his way down the cold hallway toward Stillwater Correctional Facility's visitation center. The overhead lights cast severe shadows against the gray monochromatic design.

A clerk in uniform looked up from his desk at Damian's approach. The smell of cigarettes, cheap coffee and gun powder permeated off his skin. The bags under his eyes said the clerk hadn't had nearly enough coffee to start his morning shift. Damian quickly scanned his nametag.

Garrison's eyes widened and he dropped his pen. It clinked against the hard surface and rolled off the counter with a clatter. Instead of getting up to retrieve the pen, Garrison straightened in his chair, his expression closed off. "Hello."

Damian scooped up the pen from the floor and handed it back. "I'm Detective Charming with the SPD."

"I know who you are." He snatched the pen back. "What do you want?"

Damian frowned. Why the hostility? Last time he checked, he was on good terms with the prison staff. "I'd like a copy of the visitor log for Arabia Jensen."

"Why?"

"I'm a detective with the SPD, I don't have to tell you why." Visitor logs were public record.

The man's glower remained unchanged. "That bitch lodge a complaint?"

"No." Damian tensed. "Should she?"

The guard snarled, baring coffee-stained teeth. "We didn't break any rules. We've maintained our professionalism."

And no doubt still managed to make Arabia's life miserable. Damian's blood heated. He hated that troublemaker for the mess she made, and no doubt she got what she deserved, but he also despised any mistreatment of women. He didn't want her tortured or abused. Damian paused. The guard said they maintained professionalism. That meant they weren't hurting her physically, but...but it was still wrong. It still went against everything Damian stood for. He ran a hand through his hair. Guilt hammered his brain. He was responsible for getting her arrested. He put her here.

At the time, he wanted her to suffer. But now?

He shifted his weight. His sweater itched against his skin. "Go easy on her, eh?" The words coming out of his mouth didn't sound like his own. Go easy on her? Arabia Jensen? She'd caused absolute pandemonium on the vulnerable citizens of Stillwater. Leniency and mercy were Lucy's traits, not his.

When Lucy's scumbag, absentee father tracked her down and tried to squeeze her for money, she'd demanded Damian let him go unharmed. He'd helped her as asked, but he should've killed the useless sac of a man. Not only had the deadbeat ignored his daughter her whole life, but he had the nerve to ask for money and prey on Lucy's vulnerability. She'd always wanted a father figure in her life, and after her mother's death, that need only intensified.

We should've killed him, Hippo sneered.

Damian scowled. His skin continued to itch and his griffin energy pulsed. He agreed with Hippo, and would've broken the man's neck had Lucy not turned those big, feline eyes on him and whispered, "He's still my father."

"Why?" The clerk interrupted Damian's memories. "Jensen fucked with the town."

Damian leaned down, bracing his weight on the desk with both hands. "Did your wife step out..." He glanced at the indent on the clerk's ring finger marking the location of a recently removed wedding band. "Or did you?"

The man's cheeks broke out in red blotches. Shame clouded around him like a stink bomb from his pores.

"Ah. You did." Damian pushed off the desk. "The ravenborn's actions caused a lot of hurt in town. She might deserve a prison sentence for her actions, but she doesn't deserve mistreatment. Don't let her actions affect the integrity of yours."

Again, the words felt foreign on his tongue. What the hell was happening to him? Was this because of the bonding? He never would've prattled off some psychological bullshit before. Rich words, too. If only he followed the sage advice he now apparently gave.

The guard snarled and reached below the desk to grab a page. He must've printed off the information while they spoke. He slid it across the counter. "Jensen's visitor log."

"Thank you."

Damian's phone pinged with a message as he stepped from the correctional facility and onto the sidewalk. He dug it out and read the text.

Thank you very much for replacing my window, Lucy wrote.

You're most welcome. Can I do anything else for you? Damian laughed, envisioning Lucy trying to decide whether to tell him to go fuck himself or jump off a cliff.

After a short delay, she wrote back. *You said I could pay you back. How much do I owe you?*

A date after work.

I'm not trading romantic favors for a window.

Why not?

It's not deductible as a business expense.

Damian chuckled and shook his head. *You can keep this transaction under the table. I won't tell.*

I can't believe an officer of the law is advising me to break it.

Would you rather discuss what happened on the table? Damian sucked in a breath and waited, the delay in her response excruciating.

The dots moved across his screen. Then stopped. Then started again. Then stopped and started again. Someone struggled to find her words. Finally, his phone pinged.

We can talk tonight during my repayment date.

Damian looked at the library's sign and hauled open the door. The warmth from inside rushed out and he stepped quickly into the building to shut the door behind him. He might not mind the cold, but most of Stillwater's other occupants did.

Jensen's visitor log had been understandably barren with only a few names listed. Her lawyer's name made sense, the town's frigid librarian's did not.

Why would Penelope Reed visit Arabia Jensen in prison? He could hazard a guess, but he hoped she learned something from the raven shifter between bouts of telling her off for whatever situation Penny found herself in after the love spell night.

Damian could question Arabia himself, but he needed to maintain distance from the case—especially since he was responsible for anonymously tipping off his own PD.

The smell of old books and dust flowed past him as he moved through the cocoon of the library. As far as libraries went, this one was immaculate. Usually, Damian's keen sense of smell picked up more than a little filth and dust.

The worn carpet absorbed his footsteps as he made his way to the front desk. The stagnant air muffled hush conversations and the whisper of pages turning as readers flipped through books. For a Friday morning, the place was surprisingly packed. Well, packed for a library not a football game.

A beautiful woman sat behind the solid oak desk, head down, brow furrowed, with an old book splayed open in front of her. She'd pulled her dark brown hair in a tight ponytail, which gave off a healthy sheen under the lights. Her eyelashes fluttered behind large reading glasses as she scanned the pages, and her lupine scent curled around her like an extra layer of clothing.

"Penelope."

The werewolf librarian looked up. Penelope was a striking woman. Dressed in a tight pencil skirt and silk blouse, she probably inspired tons of naughty librarian fantasies. Not for Damian, though. Only one woman provoked that kind of response in him.

He didn't just have it bad, he was ruined. He needed to make things right on their date tonight. His gut twisted in a painful knot.

"Officer Charming." Penny's eyes widened. She closed the old book and rested her hands on top of the cover, showing off her French manicure instead of the title.

He leaned forward. Parts of the title peeked out from under

her hands. The first word was definitely "Sinfully" and the last two "for More."

"Conducting some important research?"

Penny grimaced and flipped the book over to hide the cover. "How can I help you?"

"Arabia Jensen's visitor log shows you went to see her yesterday."

Penny's smile withered. She lifted her chin. "That's correct."

"Why?"

"Why?"

"Yes. Why did you go to see Arabia?"

Penny sighed and looked away. "I'd rather not say."

Ah. He understood what was going on. The whole town had been affected by Arabia's spell. "Look, Penny. I'm not interested in whatever shenanigans you got into on *that* night."

Penny whipped her head back to him. Her mouth parted, probably to pour out some sort of denial or protest.

He held his hand out for her to stop.

She clamped her mouth shut. Instead, she pulled off her reading glasses and folded them, taking the time to breathe deeply before slipping her glasses into a case on the desk.

In the rare instances their paths had crossed in the past, Penny exerted a calm, collected and controlled image when, in fact, she harbored a powerful animal inside that was the opposite of all those things. Penny snapped the glasses case shut and turned to Damian. Her gaze flashed, showing the wolf simmering beneath the surface.

Uh, oh. The quiet ones usually exploded when they finally reached their limit for putting up with shit. He'd have to tread lightly. "All I need to know is if you learned anything about the spell."

Penny folded her hands together, but couldn't hide the tension in her fingers. "Is this official police business?"

He gripped the desk with his hands. The wood creaked.

Penny leaned forward, gaze shrewd. "Is Officer Charming asking, or Damian?"

He growled.

Penny straightened with a small smirk. Cunning wolf.

"Do you really want to delve into my business, Penny? I might return the favor."

Her smile slipped away. "You really should consider a name change."

"Hardly an original comeback."

Penny pursed her lips "Why don't you ask Arabia yourself?"

That would be a hard pass. "I'm asking you."

Penny got the same look on her face as a horse about to buck. This wasn't working. Fuck.

"Why'd you wait so long?" he asked.

"Huh?"

"To see Arabia. The love spell hit the town on November seventh. Why the delay?" Hell, if he wasn't avoiding the woman, he would've stomped down there right away and demanded answers himself.

Penny's hands twisted. "Chase Baron."

"What does Arabia's lawyer have to do with your visit?"

"He blocked visitations. Probably trying to protect Arabia from all her victims."

"I doubt many would have the confidence to confront the ravenborn."

"Well, I did." Penny drew herself up in the chair. "I knew Arabia before the incident. She's not malicious or as crazy as everyone makes her out to be."

Damian leaned forward, gently casting soothing magic. "What did you find out, Penny?"

Penny sighed. The sag in her shoulders gave away the moment she decided to help. "It was some spell called Heart's

Desire."

Damian froze. No. It couldn't be. Pain wrapped around his chest and squeezed. Maybe he heard her wrong. Heart's Desire? He knew the few words he'd gleaned from the recording sounded familiar. "What?"

"According to Arabia, she only cast Heart's Desire to affect her and her lover, but something went wrong. It blasted the whole town instead. But the spell doesn't force anyone to do anything against their will."

"It freed them of any inhibitions they had from going after their heart's desire," he finished. His scalp prickled. He knew the spell. He'd never used it, obviously, but he'd heard of it. He should've recognized the lines. Lucy hadn't been magically coerced like he feared. The spell freed her from her inhibitions.

Damian was an idiot.

Penny leaned forward again. "Now, I don't want to *delve into your business*, but that look on your face tells me you have some apologizing to do."

Damian groaned.

"Don't make her wait too long." Pain flashed in her gaze.

Damian hesitated. Penny was obviously still dealing with the aftermath of that night. He reached out and placed his hand on the librarian's arm, her silk blouse smooth to the touch.

She jumped.

"It will work out," he said. Apparently, not only had he started gushing inspirational advice, but he also provided comfort and hope. What the hell? Did his bond mean he now channelled some of Lucy's personality? Huh. That might turn out a little...inconvenient. He couldn't deny the need of a positive influence sitting on his shoulder to guide him from time to time, but this could be detrimental to his health, and his job, where his ruthlessness was an asset. He snatched his hand back.

Penny's smile looked forced. "Are you saying it will work

out for me or you?"

"Both."

CHAPTER FIFTEEN

BAD FOR BUSINESS

Friday evening, December 7th

Exhaustion pulled at Lucy's limbs. Her body and mind were tired and she still reeled from Damian's last visit and his recent texts. Had she really agreed to go on a date? After work? She must've finally lost her mind. She always ended the day frazzled and smelling of stale coffee—hardly date-worthy. She needed a shower and fresh clothes.

Damian won't care, Whispurr said.

I care.

The delicious lingering scent of gingerbread from the holiday themed beverages did little to soothe her nerves. She hadn't seen him in two days and when she pressed Mateo, he revealed only that Damian had gone out of town. Her heart ached.

Well, she'd see him tonight and the anticipation was killing her last surviving nerves. The snow-filled night beckoned from the other side of the door, flashing Christmas lights taped to its metal frame. Her skin itched to shift and run, paws deep in the white powder, claws sinking into a fresh kill. She'd found snowshoe hares not just on her doorstep, but alive in the wild. They didn't naturally reside in these mountains. Had Damian brought them in for her to hunt?

Lucy sighed.

"Deep in thought?"

A man's rich voice interrupted her thoughts. Expensive cologne floated in the air around her.

She opened her eyes to find the handsome business man watching her. To be fair, she had stopped in the middle of the café, rag in one hand, cleaning bottle in the other, to close her eyes and daydream.

"I guess you could say that," she said.

The man flashed a smile. His silver hair shone, slicked with gel smelling faintly of coconuts. His well-tailored suit and immaculate presentation screamed money. He'd flirted with her for weeks. Nothing outrageous, but Lucy couldn't drum up any interest.

Things might've been different before she met Damian. Tall, fit and wearing a designer suit worth more than her rent, the man exuded confidence and reliability. Safe, yet sexy. She'd trust her investment portfolio with him.

She turned to her last and only customer and set the cleaning supplies down on a nearby table. "What is it you do again...?"

"Augustus." He stood, abandoning his coffee, and closed the distance. He held his hand out. "Augustus Reid."

She gripped his smooth hand and shook it. He hadn't answered her question. "Oh! Are you related to Penny?"

He frowned.

"Penny Reed? The librarian?"

"No."

"Oh, okay." She shrugged. Obviously, he wasn't here

visiting family for the holidays. "What brings you to Stillwater?"

"Business." He cocked his head to the side. "Actually, I wanted to discuss something with you."

Oh no. She took it back. She wouldn't trust him with her money. Not if he was one of those scam artists, offering the deal of a lifetime with infinite returns, at the low cost of her entire savings account. She scowled.

He held his hands up in mock surrender. "I'm not a salesman."

She relaxed, but only a little.

"In fact, I'm not selling anything."

She'd thought he was interested in her, or at the very least enjoyed the coffee, but turned out, this business man played a longer game. He'd buttered her up.

She straightened her spine and pulled her shoulders back. Any deal that required flirting with clients meant trouble. Or at least a bad deal.

"I want to buy your café."

Her mind blanked. "It's not for sale."

"Hear me out."

She frowned. The café closed ten minutes ago. Damian would be here soon. She wouldn't lose any business or money from listening to crazy. She may as well hear what he had to say or he'd keep badgering her. She knew the slick businessman type. The gleam in his eyes had little to do with the interior lighting and everything to do with ambition. She'd find no soft sale here.

Pffffft, like any sales pitch would get you to sell, Whispurr said, and then proceeded to clean herself.

She had no intention of selling. Her feet ached, and she wanted to see Damian and then go home to a long bath and a large glass of wine. She glanced outside again. Maybe a run in the snow, too.

She sighed. What she really wanted was more hours in the day.

"I know there's been an increase in vandalism recently. Your property value isn't going to increase in these conditions and after a certain point, it will become costly to remain in business if you're constantly patching and replacing windows." He prattled off a number.

Lucy tensed. "My café is worth more than that."

"Not with the recent break-ins and threats."

Lucy opened her mouth to argue and snapped it shut. She ran her hand along the smooth surface of the table she'd cleaned moments ago while her brain sorted through the wrongness of his comment. She narrowed her eyes. Only Tanner, Mateo and Damian knew about the note. Sure, customers could've overheard them talking, and gossip traveled fast in Stillwater, but not *that* fast. And certainly not to strangers.

Let's shift and scratch up his face, her lynx purred.

"What threats?" she asked.

The man's open and honest expression closed off.

Ah. He realized his mistake.

His gaze darkened and his handsome face turned into something more sinister. "You will sell your business to me."

Whispurr yawned. *Or what?*

Cold dark energy coiled around her. Familiar magic. The same power used in the alley to make the vandal disappear. This tainted energy confirmed Augustus' involvement in her coffee shop's vandalism—not that she needed any. His guilty face said it all. She stilled, waiting for whatever devious magic this was to pierce her skin or sink in or do whatever mambo jumbo it planned to carry out. Instead, the power curled around her as if an invisible shield held it at bay.

The businessman's brows furrowed. The black magic intensified, hammering at the barricade. He said she would sell her business to him.

Her lynx chortled.

Lucy crossed her arms over her chest and cocked a hip. "Or what?"

Her voice came out strong and unwavering. Yippee for her. This guy hopefully had no idea how freaked out she was on the inside. Her cat might be calm, but her mind reeled. She'd been attacked with magic. Magic! And somehow she'd blocked his power. She didn't possess that kind of talent. Damian was the only person she knew of with that ability.

The dark magic fell away. The man's face twisted into something truly ugly. His reaction told her all she needed to know. He was evil and she'd find out, right now, exactly how he planned to make her sell without his magic to coerce her.

And she wouldn't like the answer.

Damian clutched the steering wheel and cursed. He'd made a mess of things. The spell hadn't made Lucy sleep with him against her will. It had taken away whatever held her back from acting on her true feelings.

He was her heart's desire.

Him.

All this time, he thought the attraction was one-sided. Instead of courting Lucy the way she deserved, he'd wasted time pining for her at a distance like some love-sick schoolboy.

The wheel groaned under the pressure of his grip. If he kept this up, he'd need to replace it soon. Maybe he should get a stress ball.

He squeezed his eyes shut. He'd bonded to her. And then he'd left her. Naked and alone in the café's kitchen.

No wonder she hated him. She thought he was some douchebag who ignored her after a one-night stand. He'd make it right. He had to.

His phone vibrated. He dug it out of his pocket and accepted the call from Officer White. "Charming."

"Hey. You asked about new people in town?" White said.

"I've already eliminated Chase Baron as a suspect."

"Not him. You also asked about a businessman with gray hair. I found him. His name's Augustus Reid. Romeo-Echo-India-Delta. Silverfox. No known supernatural abilities. Has a bunch of the women in town drooling all over him. He arrived prior to the florist shop vandalism. He recently purchased the office building on the corner of Main Street."

The image of the businessman lingering in the café popped into Damian's head. First, he thought the man was in league with Arabia to vandalize the café. Then he thought the man was a flirt and possible competition for Lucy's affection. Now it turned out, his first instinct might've been correct all along. Minus Arabia's involvement.

"Thanks, White. I'll look into it."

"No problem." The officer hung up.

Damian would look into it, all right. After he fixed things with Lucy. She'd met his courting efforts these last two weeks with indifference, and he hadn't seen her in two days. His chest ached. Leaving Stillwater to track down her father had been agony. At least he knew Earl May wasn't involved.

This date was his chance to lay all his feelings for Lucy on the table and make things right between them. With that thought, Lucy's kitchen counter popped into his memory, along with vivid images from that night. Damian sucked in a breath and gripped the cool door handle. The incomplete mating bond flared around his heart and squeezed.

He popped open the SUV door and stepped into the night. Fluffy, thick snowflakes drifted down and settled on his winter jacket. He lifted his face to the moon, barely visible behind the clouds. A perfect night for hunting. Maybe Lucy would join him for a run.

Don't get ahead of yourself, Charming, Hippo said.

Thanks for the pep talk.

Hippo growled. *You're such a thick-skulled idiot. You should've fixed this a long time ago.*

You're right.

His griffin's beak snapped shut and feathers fluffed out.

Damian turned to the café, still lit up, and crossed the street. Even though it was after close, he knew to look for her here and not at home for their date.

He took a deep breath and pulled the door open. Lucy's familiar scent welcomed him—mischief and mayhem, wrapped in sugar—but this time the scent came laced with something else. Something off. He couldn't put a finger on it.

Augustus Reid stood in front of Lucy, his back to the door and both hands bracing against the counter to cage Lucy between his designer-clad arms. Was she one of the women in town drooling all over him?

"She's closed," Augustus snarled over his shoulder.

Did she forget their plans? Or was this some sort of twisted setup with the sole purpose of hurting him? Ice traveled through his veins. Damian took a deep breath and pushed the prickly sensation away. Lucy was many things, but cruel wasn't one of them. He couldn't see her face. He studied the man instead. His body language was possessive.

And wrong. Dark energy pulsed around them.

Damian narrowed his eyes and let the door close behind him. "Like hell she is."

Augustus stepped back and turned to him.

Relief washed over Lucy's face. "Damian."

Understanding clicked. Damian hadn't interrupted a love tryst between his mate and the smarmy businessman. Augustus Reid had been trying to do something else. Intimidate her? Threaten her? Whatever the man intended, Lucy didn't like it. Augustus Reid made his mate uneasy and that meant he'd pay.

Hippo shrieked.

"What have you done?" Damian curled up his lip and stepped forward.

A wall of magic, reeking of dark, twisted curses slammed against him. It crashed over his skin, useless and harmless, his griffin essence creating a protective shield from the magic. The power pulsed around him.

"What I've done is none of your business," Augustus said.

The magic pressed against Damian's barrier. Poking and prodding, but finding no holes in the defense. What the hell was this guy? Warlock? Demon? Some sort of hybrid?

Augustus' expression twisted.

Damian brushed the magic off. "I disagree."

"What the hell is wrong with this town?"

Damian's power pulsed. He pushed it down. He didn't need magic to deal with this guy. "Lucy isn't interested in whatever you're offering."

Augustus' frown eased away and he smiled. "I haven't been here long, but I've been here long enough to know she wants nothing to do with you, either."

Damian rocked back on his heels. "That might be true, but you still need to come with me."

Augustus snorted. "Are you here to save her?"

Lucy's eyebrows shot up, and her hands balled into fists.

Damian laughed, more at Lucy's expression than the man's words. He identified the tang to her scent—rage and determination. She might be scared of this asshole, but she had no plans to play the victim tonight.

"You're an idiot if you think Lucy needs saving."

Augustus frowned and turned back to Lucy.

Whack!

Her fist connected flush with his jaw. Augustus' head snapped to the side and he staggered back.

Lucy's pouty lips twisted into a ferocious snarl.

His mate was beautiful. He wanted to rip this man to shreds and press Lucy against the blood spattered walls to show her exactly how sorry he was.

Damian closed the distance, his boots hitting the tile in hard, fast steps. She'd never go for that. She'd insist on cleaning up first.

Augustus recovered and turned to Lucy. Before he could attack, Damian grabbed one of his baby smooth hands, then the other and wrenched them behind his back.

He touched our mate. His griffin pressed against his skin. *Destroy him.*

He squeezed his eyes shut. With one swift move, he could snap this guy's neck and bury him in the woods where no one would find him. His nauseating scent laced with overdone cologne still coated Lucy's wrists like an unwanted film of dirt.

Damian snarled.

Lightning struck outside, sending blinding white light flashing through the café. A boom of thunder shook the building. An unnatural storm brewed outside in response to Damian's rage.

Lucy's hand gripped his arm. "Remember your job," she whispered, tone light and soothing.

"To hell with my job," he growled. "He threatened you."

"How will you afford your caffeine addiction if you don't have a job to support your habit?" she asked.

A surprised bark of laughter escaped his chest and the tension from his griffin's demands eased. He leaned in as he fastened the cuffs with satisfying clicks around Augustus' wrists. "I'm arresting you for vandalism and issuing threats."

Augustus laughed. "My lawyers will have me out in an hour."

Damian released his griffin energy, surrounding Augustus and letting it smother the other man. "I sincerely hope they do," Damian said. "It's a perfect night for hunting."

Augustus stiffened. He had no idea how close he came to dying moments ago.

"This way." Damian shoved him toward the door and read him his rights. When he reached the exit, he turned to Lucy.

She'd remained by the counter. Her expression soft and open. The cold veneer had cracked.

"Are you okay?" he asked.

She smiled, teeth flashing under lighting. "Better now."

"We have a date. Will you wait for me?"

Her beautiful feline eyes widened. Did she honestly think he'd abandon their date so easily?

"I'll be about an hour. We need to talk."

Augustus groaned. "Lock me up, but don't make me listen to this."

Damian kneed him in the hamstring.

Augustus grunted and his leg buckled.

"Lucy?" Damian asked.

She chewed her bottom lip.

"Please?"

She rubbed her arms and looked away. Her cheeks flushed a beautiful rosy red. "Okay."

Her body language spoke of uncertainty and unease, but he'd take it. He'd take anything she gave. He needed to make it right between them.

CHAPTER SIXTEEN

CATNIP

Lucy eyed the snow filled night, her locked café's door at her back, and the empty street in front. Regret soaked into her weary muscles. Too late for a run now. She'd waited two hours for Damian to return. He seemed so sincere when he asked her to wait. She wanted to believe him. She wanted to believe something came up or somehow booking Augustus Reid took longer than expected.

Did you see his face when he arrested that asshole? Whispurr asked. *He'll be here.*

She huffed, breath forming little puffs of condensed air.

An engine revved in the distance.

Lucy looked up.

Damian's SUV swerved around the corner and the vehicle barreled down the road toward her, spraying more snow on the sidewalks. The detective had many talents, but driving fast was not one of them. She bit her lip and swallowed the giggle.

My, my, my. Someone's in a hurry.

For her.

Damian Charming, the calm and collected—bordering cold

and dismissive—detective raced to return to her. A smile tugged at her lips. The weight pulling her heart down to her stomach relented, and her chest expanded.

The SUV slid to a stop at a safe distance in front of her.

Damian leapt out of the vehicle. "I'm sorry. That took longer than I expected. Things kept popping up when I thought I'd get away. I would've texted otherwise."

"It's okay." Lucy's own words surprised her. It was okay? Yes, it really was.

"I know it's too late for a date now." Damian straightened. "Can I at least offer you a ride?"

She nodded, while her mind made a dirty play on words.

"Where's your toque? It's cold out."

Lucy straightened, her smile genuine. "My toque?"

"I speak Canadian," he said, tone indignant.

Damian beat her to the passenger door, his winter boots crunching in the snow, and held it open. She slipped into the smooth seat and sniffed the cold air. His vehicle smelled like him—potent and powerful. She relaxed into the cool leather.

Damian shut the door gently and jogged around to the other side.

Aside from their night of uninhibited sexcapades, she'd never seen the cool and collected detective so unsettled.

She did this, she realized. Her. She made Mr. High and Mighty lose control.

Lucy suppressed a smile.

Damian turned to her, golden eyes flashing like lightning across a thunderous night sky.

Oh my.

She might've unsettled him, but his impact on her was just as potent.

Only a foot separated them. The silky black hair she'd gripped in the throes of passion teased her an arm's length away. She could reach out and touch him right now. The space inside the vehicle narrowed. The air grew thin.

Damian's gaze flicked to her lips. His breathing slowed to match hers. Every breath she released, he inhaled, as if it fed more than his lungs.

She clutched her purse on her lap and held her breath.

"I'll take you home," he said with a tone that implied he'd rather do something else.

Yes, home. She needed to go home and sleep. Except... Except, suddenly the idea she'd clung to moments ago didn't seem so appealing anymore.

"I don't want to go home."

Damian leaned in. "Want to go for a run?"

Tempting, but that involved clothing removal and even if she changed somewhere else, running as a lynx beside a powerful griffin made her vulnerable. She wasn't sure she was ready to show Damian any more vulnerability yet.

She glanced outside. It really was a great night for a run. "Not tonight."

"Where do you want to go, then?"

"Let's talk at your place." She stressed the word "talk," but the slow smile spreading across Damian's face made her rethink her decision. Should she change her mind? Her heart sped up at the idea of what could happen, but she wanted the ability to *leave*. Damian had already left her once, she couldn't bear for him to walk away again.

If she didn't like what he had to say, she could walk home. He didn't live far from her. She looked him up. If anyone ever asked, though, she'd deny knowledge of this information and how she obtained it.

"My place it is," Damian said.

"To talk."

He nodded, not quite wiping the smile off his face. "To talk."

He navigated the SUV from the curb and drove them to

their neighborhood in silence. Neither of them lived far from the café, which is why Lucy often walked to work. That and she loved fresh air. She only drove if the weather was truly miserable or if she was bone-numbingly tired.

Damian parked in front of a modest, two-story home, more "normal" than she expected for a griffin. She always imagined him sitting on top of pile of gold in an over-the-top mansion.

Or was that dragons?

She shrugged. She never cared for shiny things. She needed forests, rabbits, and room to roam.

Damian held the door to his home open and she stepped inside. Beautifully inlaid stonework greeted her in the entranceway, which opened to an opulent room completely defying the plain exterior. Expensive furnishings, glittering chandeliers and tasteful artwork adorned the house. Her jaw dropped open.

Wait a minute. She mentally estimated the size of the room. The home she viewed from the street couldn't possibly be large enough to contain this inside space. He must have spelled the exterior somehow to make it appear smaller.

"Do you like it?" Damian asked.

"Yes."

Damian's serious expression cracked into a smile. He closed the door and reached past her to flick on the lights, though neither of them needed it. He peeled off his jacket and held his hand out for hers. She shucked off her boots and handed her coat to Damian. While he put the jackets away and took off his boots, she moved into the house. The artificial light reflected off clean surfaces. A large crystal statue sat in a display nook, illuminated with its own special light. Mesmerized, Lucy walked toward it.

The artist skillfully captured the spirit and physicality of a lynx stepping from a halo of ice. With a fluffy winter coat, the wild animal called to her from its poised position, as if at any moment, it would continue its sleek movement out of the cave to join her in a hunt. The radiance and majesty of the lynx shone through the sparkling crystal.

Lucy's breath caught. Is this how Damian saw her?

"I like shiny things." Damian's voice teased her ears and his breath fanned her hair. He stood so close behind her.

She could turn around and be in his arms in a second. "I'm sure there's plenty of other crystal statues."

"I wanted this one."

I want you, he meant. His feelings so clear and unshielded in his voice she swore she heard his thoughts. She turned to find him inches away, gaze serious and intent. His T-shirt stretched over his tense muscles, as if on the verge of action. He wanted a lynx statue, not a griffin as she'd expect from an arrogant beast. But, as she continuously discovered, Damian wasn't what he seemed, and yet, he was more.

"Do you have a name for your lynx?" he asked.

"Whispurr," she answered, her cheeks growing hot.

His eyebrows rose. She'd surprised him, again.

"I was ten when I named her. Not exactly the poster-child for maturity."

He ran a finger down the edge of the statue. "It's a good name. It suits you. You're a silent predator."

"Wh...what do you call yours?" she stammered. Why did her heart ache?

"Hippo."

If she'd been drinking, Damian's face would be coated with the drink and spit. "Hippo?"

"Short for Hippogriff. I've never told anyone that before."

That couldn't be right. Not the secrecy part, but the name. "Isn't a hippogriff half eagle half horse?

"Absolutely."

"Then...?"

"I needed to call this mulish bird something to put him in

his place." He tapped his forehead. "It stuck."

A giggle bubbled up from her chest. Her lynx preened.

"Did you bring snowshoes to our forest?" she asked. To anyone else, her statement would take on a different meaning.

Damian nodded.

Her heart melted and her head grew light. Was this swooning? Nope. No. Stay strong. Naked on the counter. Naked. "You wanted to talk?"

"Yes, would you like something to drink?"

Yes. Something hard. And stiff. And with those two thoughts, her mind spiraled into the gutter. What was wrong with her? "No, thank you."

He nodded and waved at a couch set.

She folded her arms. Like hell she was sitting for this. She needed to stand for a quick escape, thank you. She probably should've left her jacket and boots on.

His mouth turned down. "The night we..."

She rose an eyebrow.

He cleared his throat. "The night we were together, a member of our community unleashed a powerful spell."

"Arabia's love spell."

Damian grunted.

"I don't live under a rock."

He grimaced and continued. "I'm fairly immune to magical influences, so it took me a while to realize you'd been spelled."

Lucy frowned. She'd felt a number of things that night, none of them bad or unwelcomed.

"I was horrified when I realized you'd acted under a spell, that you'd been an unwilling participant."

"So you bolted."

"It goes against everything I am and stand for to take advantage of someone without the ability to say no," he said.

"So you left me naked on my kitchen island. Not the best reaction."

"I'm sorry, Lucy." He looked away and started to pace. "I shouldn't have left you. I thought you'd hate me and I'd be the last person you'd want to see in the morning."

"So you stayed away instead of talking to me about it." At first, her gut twisted, like unease ate her belly from the inside, but the discomfort dissipated, replaced with warmth blossoming in her chest. She'd misread his actions entirely.

He stopped pacing and turned to her. "Another poor choice."

"That's putting it kindly," she said. "You made a bunch of bad decisions."

"I know you think poorly of me, Lucy." He reached for her hands. They dwarfed her own. "I'm trying to show you I'm capable of more."

Is that what the presents were for? The offers of kindness? The preening? To show his worthiness?

She whispered, "I wasn't unwilling."

Damian's gaze sparked like living flames. He squeezed her hands. "I discovered the exact nature of the spell. Do you want to know what it is?"

Lucy jerked her chin up and down, not trusting her mouth to form words.

"The spell is a long one, but this is the important part: *Freedom from slavery, naked in your rites. Liberated from fear and doubt this night. Before the dawn, deliver my heart's delight and desire.*"

The words echoed in her mind, familiar yet foreign. "But what does it mean? I didn't think Arabia's spell affected me at all."

"It did, but it only released you from your inhibitions, from whatever stopped you from seeking your heart's desire."

Lucy's breathing hitched. Heat crept up her neck and face. She already knew she wanted Damian. She always assumed he didn't want her, but the expression on his face right now stole her breath away. A little smug, prideful...and happy?

He released her and ran his hands up her arms. "I assumed the spell didn't work on me because of my natural defense against magic, but maybe the true reason the spell didn't fully work on me is that the only inhibition I had from pursuing you was I thought you didn't like me."

"Quite the opposite."

"Apparently."

She bit her lip and looked away from the intensity of his gaze. He was her own personal catnip. She couldn't resist him if she tried. His vibrating energy called to her own and she wanted to lick him up and savor the flavor.

"Tell me I haven't fucked this up," he said, voice low.

"Oh, you've messed up pretty well."

"Tell me I haven't fucked this up so much, it's irreparable. Lucy, I want you. More than anything. I always have. If I could rewind time and—"

She stopped his words by planting her mouth on his.

Damian groaned, a low manly sound, and kissed her back. He wrapped his strong arms around her and pulled her in, smothering her against his chest, his shirt soft. His hands roamed, all the while drinking her in as if she fed his soul. Maybe she did. She certainly felt more alive with this one kiss than she had for the last few weeks without him.

She pulled back. "What about me being a lynx?"

Damian straightened, his expression puzzled. "What about it?"

"Isn't it beneath you?"

"I want you beneath me." He growled and reached for her.

She slipped from his arms, though desire shot through her body.

"Or you can be on top." Damian's smile grew.

A memory of her riding him on top of her kitchen counter crashed into her mind. Head back, body arched, with Damian's mouth on her breast. Her body ached for him.

She took a couple of steps away, not trusting herself this close to so much charm. Ah. Charming. Now he fit his surname perfectly. "When you helped drive my father from town and out of my life..." She dropped down her voice. "You said I was ridiculous and should leave it to someone more *capable*."

Damian's smile disappeared.

Sure, on a basic level she understood Damian was more equipped to handle situations like the one involving her father. It wasn't that he was wrong, it was how he said it and what he revealed. His words implied lynx shifters were inferior. How could she be with someone so dismissive of her own people? Of her? "You made me feel insignificant and little."

"You *are* little."

She pursed her lips.

Damian ground his teeth. "Physically, you're a lot smaller than I am, both in human and in animal form. You're also without additional magic. Not only can I shift into a griffin, but I can also wield magic. Your lynx is magnificent, but as far as physical prowess and fighting abilities go, hunting snowshoe hares isn't a skill that gives you a glowing recommendation for taking out a manipulator hell-bent on extracting money from his estranged, biological daughter through whatever means necessary. He didn't play fair, Luce. When preying on your vulnerability and desire for a father-figure didn't work, he tried to spell you. He planned to abduct you. The last thing we needed to do was deliver you to that psycho dressed up in a pretty bow."

"So I'm pathetic *and* dumb, now?" Her muscles tensed. "Do I not have any intelligence or ability to stay out of harm's way?"

"You're amazing. You're hard-working. Dedicated. Loyal. Powerful and fierce. I love watching you hunt. You're the most beautiful thing in the world. And the most precious. You were vulnerable and I didn't and don't want to see you hurt."

Her chest expanded. Her mind cleared and all thoughts of Damian's dismissive attitude fled. "So you said I was ridiculous because...?"

"Because I wanted you to let me handle it. I *am* better equipped for those sorts of things."

"And you didn't want me getting hurt."

"I wanted to protect you." Damian's gaze darkened.

Lucy sighed. "I asked for your help, not your protection."

Damian shook his head. "Regardless of whether you asked or not, I *will* ensure your safety, Lucy. I'll go to any means to protect you. It's not within me to leave the person I love vulnerable to attack."

Her breath caught. Had he just said that? He was in love with her? Her chest expanded. So light on her feet, if she spread her arms right now, she'd probably fly.

"You need to work on your delivery. Your words hurt me."

"I know. I'm sorry."

Two apologies from the mighty griffin in one evening. My, my. Maybe she should go for a third? She took two steps forward to close the distance between them and slid her hands up his chest and neck until they rested along his jaw and the sides of his face. Without a word, she rose on her toes and kissed him again.

He groaned and pulled her tight against his body. The world around her faded. All that existed was Damian and how his body touched hers, how his mouth played, his tongue teased and his hands roamed.

He lifted her and she locked her legs around his waist, his muscles rippling against her inner thighs with each step. He carried her through the house and up a flight of stairs. Her nerves sang. If only he'd move *faster*.

Damian sprinted up the last couple of steps and barged

through his bedroom door. Had he heard her wishes? Her body's demands?

He placed her gently on a thick duvet that billowed around her, sending a delicious cloud of his scent into the air. He peeled off her clothes and kissed every inch of skin exposed with the slow removal of soft fabric. The material tormented her already singing nerves. She pulled his head down to hers and kissed him back.

With long, unhurried strokes, he caressed her body. His hands leaving her briefly to strip off his clothes. They fell to the floor. He stretched beside her, huge and muscular. Waves of his magic pressed against her skin and he reached for her again. Anticipation raced through her veins.

She belonged in his arms with his tongue in her mouth, his hands exploring her body. He belonged inside her. Need pulsed. The ache intensified. She ground against him.

Tonight wasn't about a spell or the frenzied meeting of two people hooking up. Tonight was about them, and how they shared the same potent feelings for each other. She couldn't get enough of him and didn't want to wait one second longer.

Damian chuckled silently against her lips. He rolled them over so he pinned her to the cloud of fluffy bedding with his hard body. He flexed his hips and pressed against her. She rose to meet him. With delicious slowness, he pushed inside, his gaze molten as he watched her. Full and aching, he stretched her.

Yes. This.

He belonged here like this.

His lips tasted the skin along her neck. He began to move, making love to her until the room disappeared and she got lost in the rhythm of their bodies and the building ache he fed.

CHAPTER SEVENTEEN

JEWEL THIEF

Damian carefully extracted himself from the tangle of silken limbs and slipped from the warmth of Lucy's body. Her alluring scent curled around him, fusing with his own and pressing against his pulse—Lucy's mate claim. For the first time in his life, true happiness expanded his chest and made him weightless. His bare feet hit the cold floor and he stretched in the dark room, illuminated only by streaks of moonlight through the blinds.

She was here and she was his. All he needed now was to complete the matching ritual and present her with the gold bead. Although only the size of a large pearl, the bauble was infused with his essence. Damian had waited a long time to give his mating bead to someone.

To Lucy.

He padded down the steps to the living room. The chill in the air caressed his skin. He flicked the switch for the gas fireplace. Clicking echoed through the house and the fireplace roared to life. The glow bathed his skin. The cold might not bother him, but it affected Lucy.

He turned to the side table. The light from the fire flickered and danced along the gold embellishments of a decorative box sitting prominently on the maple-stained surface. He lifted the lid.

The black velvet padding on the inside of the box stared back at him. Empty.

How could this be? Where was the gold bead? He didn't leave it anywhere else. This wasn't some trinket haphazardly left around. Someone must've taken it. Damian froze. Someone *stole* from him. Rage gripped him. His griffin energy lashed out and thrashed against his skin.

Someone stole from his horde.

Magic swelled. His arms and legs shook. The thief hadn't taken just any article from his horde. They took his magically infused mating bauble.

Damian dropped his head back and screeched.

The walls shook. Lucy bolted upright in bed. A piercing cry from an eagle shattered the stillness of the night. What the hell?

Damian thundered up the stairs and into the bedroom. He stood at the entrance, gaze wild, expression livid, completely naked, large and imposing. Cool air from downstairs rushed in with him and the moonlight danced along his taut muscles. He vibrated with anger, and the air grew spicy with his enraged scent.

"What's wrong?"

Damian took a number of deep breaths before answering. "Someone stole from me."

Who the heck would be dumb enough to steal from a detective? A griffin detective? The action screamed recklessness. "What did they steal?"

"A gold bead."

"Grand Theft Bauble?" Laughter died in her throat when she saw his ferocious expression. Okay, then. No making fun of the gold bead. She cleared her throat. "A bead?"

He nodded. "I had the bauble in a jewelry box in the living room and now it's gone. The thief, whomever they are, will pay."

"What's the big deal? It's a bead, isn't it?"

He heaved deep breaths. His griffin energy crackled around him, raising the hairs on her arms and tingling her nerves. A walking lightning bolt, his power surrounded him like a small thunderstorm. Should she hide? Duck and cover? Board some windows? Not much point when the storm was already inside.

The vibrations settled and Damian's breathing slowed. He reined in his power, breath by breath, visible calm settling over his tense muscles.

"It's not *just* a bead," he said.

She sat up straighter in bed, the sheet slipped from her body.

Damian stilled. His gaze raked her body. "This bauble is infused with my essence, part of who I am. It contains my magic."

"Like a horcrux?"

"This isn't a middle grade fictional story about underage wizards."

She shrugged. Obviously, this was a big deal to him, but she had no idea why.

"When griffins reach maturity, we go on a journey, very similar to the raven shifters' Launching. After male griffins complete their travels, we create a bauble using our magical essence. This bead represents the first item of our horde, and after bonding, we give—"

"After bonding?" Her mind reeled. After bonding? After? As in *post bond*.

You're a quick one, Whispurr said.

Did you know about this?

Silence.

Answer me, dammit! When did this happen? How did I not notice? Whispurr!

More silence.

Ugh. Cats. They didn't obey commands. The fickle beasts only cared when it suited them.

Damian raked a hand through his hair and looked away. The floor creaked under his shifting weight.

"When did you bond to me?" She tried to keep her voice light and calm, but even she heard the waver. Could it really be true? Was he all hers? Forever? She picked up a corner of the sheet and played with the edge. *Stay calm, stay calm.*

"Our first night together," Damian answered.

The sheet slipped from her fingers and her lynx's puns and cackling faded to the background. His magic. She'd felt the potent energy that night, caressing and sheathing her with its delicious thrumming. She'd pulled in the power, or it consumed her. Either way, she'd accepted the magic, as she accepted Damian.

Whispurr puffed up and pranced around her brain. *He accepted you, too.*

Lucy's scent coated every inch of his body, marking him for all to see, or smell, that he belonged to her. She'd mated with him in every possible way. Why was she surprised he did the same?

Because you still think you're not worthy, Whispurr said.

I'm not.

Pshhhhhht! He can't resist the pussy, Whispurr head-butted her brain. *Get it? Get it? Because you're a pussy...cat and you have a—*

Please stop.

Girl, you stop. We're perfect for him, and he thinks so, too.

He wouldn't have bonded to you otherwise.

Holy crap.

A griffin bonded with her.

No wonder Augustus' magic wouldn't work on her.

"My *bauble* is for my mate and bride. For you. Not a thief. Just as my horde, and all that I am is yours. This is what the bead represents, and why it's so important for *you* to have it."

Her brain couldn't keep up. Love, bonding, now marriage. She should freak out, yet...yet everything felt so right. "Is this a marriage proposal?"

Damian scowled. "It would've been had my property not been stolen."

"Come back to bed. You bonded to me. There's no higher commitment than that. I don't need a bauble. I need you."

He hesitated. "I need you, too. But..."

"But?"

He squeezed his eyes shut. His griffin raged inside, demanding release. "I need to get my bauble back."

"Words I never thought I'd hear a grown man say."

"It's a griffin thing."

Her eyebrows rose. She picked up the edge of the sheet and pulled it up to cover herself again.

"I *need* you to have it." He stalked to the door. His footsteps fell heavy against the floor. "And I can't allow someone to steal from me."

"Don't leave me," she whispered. "Again."

Damian froze with his hand on the doorknob. Her pain drifted in the air with her scent. It was the "again" that cut him. His griffin screeched. He turned around.

The glow from the moon outside illuminated his mate like a wind sprite sitting in the clouds; in reality, she sat alone in his giant bed. Small, naked, and clutching the sheet to her chest like a flimsy film of protection.

Damian cursed. "I'm an idiot."

"You're only figuring that out now?" Her words held heart and sass, but her body language still screamed vulnerability. A wisp of her soft hair slipped down her shoulder.

Damian would do anything to make her feel safe and secure. He needed to reassure his mate of his sincerity and trustworthiness, and he still had a lot of ground to make up after his earlier mistakes.

He'd retrieve his property tomorrow.

And he knew just where to look, or rather, who to look at as a suspect.

But tonight...Tonight he'd use everything in his considerable arsenal to wipe that look of uncertainty from his mate's face and the hurt of abandonment from her heart.

CHAPTER EIGHTEEN

RANSACKING THE RAVEN'S NEST

Saturday, December 8th

Damian tossed clothes from the dresser. It had to be here. But it wasn't. With each shirt, his temper rose. Arabia's bedroom lay in shambles. He'd ripped through the mattress and thrown it on its side, the bedding lay in a messy heap on the floor and clothes littered the entire room. If Arabia wanted him to care about her personal belongings, she shouldn't have stolen from him.

It wasn't here. Goddammit.

Arabia's bold scent clung to every surface. The faint hint of wolf also drifted in the air. Her last guest had been a werewolf. Her lawyer or someone else? Along with the scents, the tease of his bead's magical essence lingered in the cold, empty cabin like a sweet aftertaste. It wasn't here, but it had been at one point, and long enough to leave an impression.

Damian peeled something clinging to his shirt. Red panties...Ugh. Damian flung the sexy garment away from him.

He wasn't a prude, but the only woman's underwear he was interested in seeing or playing with were Lucy's. He only went through Arabia's stuff out of necessity.

And desperation.

With Arabia's court date looming near, he didn't need his involvement with the case scrutinized, especially not with her lawyer lover, Chase Baron, digging into every possible lead. The smallest technicalities got cases thrown out of court all the time. An off-duty SPD detective using police-issue surveillance equipment to illegally monitor a private citizen and then calling in the crime anonymously wasn't a small technicality. It was career-ending huge.

The risk of coming here to search for his bead was worth it. He needed to find the bauble for Lucy. He'd risk everything for her.

His phone vibrated in his pocket. He pulled it out and stomped into Arabia's kitchen without turning on the lights. He could see well enough at night and didn't want anyone to notice the glow of cabin lights when the occupant was known to be in jail awaiting trial. Like the living room, he'd ripped everything apart, thrown open drawers, doors, cupboards and closets and rummaged through the contents with little care for retribution. Like hell he'd put any of this back. He'd cloaked himself and magically obscured his fingerprints so the only evidence he'd leave was a hint of his scent, nothing else would incriminate him, but right now criminal charges were the farthest from his mind. He came up empty handed. No bead.

"Charming," he answered his phone.

"Has anyone ever told you how ironic your last name is?" Mateo asked.

Repeatedly. "I can be charming when I need to be."

Silence stretched.

"Baron isn't our guy," Mateo said.

"Yeah, I know. He arrived too late to commit the earlier

vandalism."

Mateo grunted.

"I meant to text you. How'd you figure it out?" Lucy proved very distracting in the best way possible. Comforting pressure bloomed in his chest. He needed to complete the mating ceremony.

"Yeah, uh..."

Damian waited. This would be good. Though Mateo wasn't exactly a man of many words, the ones he did use tended to be strong and confident.

"I overheard Baron talking with the District Attorney at the Clover Club."

"Why do you sound sheepish?"

"They might've mentioned Mrs. Bee's broken awning."

Damian barked out a laugh. He knew exactly who was responsible for that damage.

Mateo hung up.

Damian laughed harder. He slid his phone into his pocket and walked through the small corridor and laundry room, his footsteps echoed in the cabin. He approached the back entrance and opened the door. Heavy snow fell on the silent forest and field surrounding Arabia's cabin. He'd flown here in griffin form, not wanting his vehicle spotted heading to or from Jensen's home and used his magic to unlock the back door.

Unlike other shifters, he kept his clothing and belongings when he transformed as long as he wore something to begin with. But sometimes not all his things came back with him. Over the years, he'd lost a number of possessions. He still had no idea where his stuff went while he tramped around in griffin form, but that was the beauty of magic. It didn't have to make sense. Because...magic.

If he had a choice, though, he preferred to be naked for a shift instead of encumbered with restrictive clothing. He enjoyed how truly free he felt in the blissful moment of transformation when he shed his humanity and embraced his true self.

He closed his eyes and called on the fiery power. It coated his skin and the area around him. Potent and electrifying, the griffin form slid through his body and replaced his human form. He screeched into the night—the piercing cry of an eagle, but louder and deeper. Time to go home to Lucy. Empty handed.

He pumped his wings and launched into the night sky. The cold air pressed against his wings.

Aside from the magical residue, he didn't sense the bauble's energy anywhere in the house. Arabia must have the bead on her somehow. Maybe he could get into the correctional facility's vault.

Of course, he hadn't sensed the bead on Arabia the last few times he ran into her after their date, either, but he hadn't been looking for it and the ravenborn had their own cloaking magic.

Well, he was searching now. He had to find a way to get his bead from Arabia without alerting her lawyer or setting off the entire correctional facility's alarms.

Damian stepped from the inky night and into the headlights of Lucy's parked car. He'd received a text from her earlier in the day to meet him here. It was one of his favorite hunting spots. This high in the mountains, the snow hadn't let up and fell in heavy flakes. Lucy stepped from the open driver's door and walked to meet him. "It might be easier—"

Her nose twitched. She stopped walking and frowned.

"What's wrong?"

"I'm not sure. Do I want to know why you smell like another woman?" Her cheeks flushed.

"Are you jealous?"

The red deepened.

Damian chuckled. "You have nothing to worry about."

"Is that so?"

"You're the one I want, Luce." How could she doubt him now after what they shared?

"I heard you went out on a date with Arabia." The color of her cheeks deepened to an almost purple color. "But that was months ago, wasn't it?"

Damian laughed. "Yeah, and the most uneventful date ever. I couldn't stop thinking about you."

"Your words are sweet, but you're not explaining why you smell like her now. Isn't she in jail?" Her gaze raked over him again. She let out a long breath, a white puff of air in the cold mountain night. "What did you do?"

"I searched her house."

"Why?"

The most adorable wrinkle of skin folded between her eyebrows. Should he tell her that?

"Damian." Her hands balled into fists. The snow crunched under her feet and her muscles tensed. Would she pounce on him if he refused to answer? Maybe he should remain quiet and see what happened...

Lucy barred her teeth.

No. Better not. "Arabia and I went on a date a while ago. One date with no chemistry and it went nowhere."

"As much as I love dwelling on your previous relationships, we already covered this. Stop stalling."

"I cooked her dinner."

Lucy's scowl froze. Her gaze flashed.

"She was in my house, Luce."

Her mouth twisted, and for a second it looked as though she'd bolt. She relaxed and rocked back. Her expression softened. "You think she stole your bauble?"

"I know she did."

"How?"

"Griffin," he explained.

She waited and folded her arms.

"The bead left magical residue in her home."

"How'd you know to look there in the first place?"

"I've met enough ravenborn in my lifetime to know of their obsession with shiny things and getting into trouble."

"Exactly how old are you?"

He winked, but his blood still boiled. He couldn't get Arabia's waggling finger wave from replaying in his mind. "I had the bead stored away from sight, but I wouldn't put it past her to go snooping when I left her in the living room alone. She was the only one to step foot in my house invited, at least recently, and the uninvited would've come up against my wards."

"You sound pretty sure of her guilt. If you only found residue, maybe one of her guests had your bauble."

"Are you defending her? She cast the Heart's Desire spell over the whole town."

"Allegedly." She used air quotes.

"Lucy." He hesitated. He needed to tell her the truth, even if she might bolt. "I know she's guilty because I had her place bugged and I'm the one who anonymously called it in."

Lucy's mouth gaped open. It closed and reopened a couple of more times.

"Try to use your nice words," he suggested.

She glared at him. "Is that even legal?"

"Of course not." His chest constricted.

Lucy's mouth hung open again.

"Still want me?"

"Absolutely," she said without hesitation.

Damian relaxed.

"But you need to learn some social etiquette and...I don't know...morals?"

"Griffin," he said as way of an explanation again.

"Exactly. Behave." She pulled her shirt over her head. No bra. The moonlight played with the curves of her full breasts. The snow drifted down to land on her smooth skin and melted on impact.

The anger fled, chased away by a different kind of heat. He stepped forward. "Griffin's aren't exactly well known for behaving."

"Uh-uh!" She waved her finger at him. "Run first."

He growled and lunged.

Lucy squeaked and dodged. She pulled down her jogging pants, exposing neon blue Brazilian cut panties.

"If you wanted to run first, you shouldn't have worn those."

"Don't you dare. These are my favorites."

He smiled and stalked forward. She definitely should've worn different underwear. He'd buy her new ones.

With a defiant glare, Lucy started her shift as she pulled off her underwear. God, that looked painful. With her teeth barred, and eyes scrunched, Lucy folded in on herself and fell to the snow-dusted ground. Bones cracked and crunched. Fur materialized and new skin formed.

Damian had always been proud of his griffin abilities, maybe too proud, but now he was thankful for his painless, magical shift.

He squashed the urge to gather his mate in his arms. He knew better than to touch her in the transition stage. The contact with the raw, transforming tissue would be excruciating.

A couple of minutes later, minutes that felt like years, Lucy stood on four fluffy paws and shook the remnants of the change from her thick winter coat.

His griffin pushed at his skin. Now he could go to her. Drawing inward, he called on his magic and let the tingling transformation consume him. Once shifted, the world became clearer, his eagle eyes taking everything in with crystalline precision. His mate glowed as she stood waiting in front of him.

Oh, they'd run first, but once they were back in human shape, he had plans for his little lynx.

Lucy barked at him and took off, spraying him with a thin blanket of powder. He launched after her and gave chase.

The run didn't last long. Lucy was either tired or just as distracted by his presence as he was with hers. He caught her in his arms the moment her shift ended, sending them both into the snow. Her naked back pressed into his chest. He pulled her up, mouth clamped on her silken neck to taste the sweetness of her skin. She remained on her hands and knees and arched her back, pressing her butt into him.

He pushed into her heat. Slow and steady, he savored every inch he claimed. She moaned and pressed back, demanding more.

God, he loved the sounds she made.

He should go slowly, but he couldn't. He lost all control when he was inside her. The mating frenzy was still hot and singing in his veins. He gripped her hips and thrust into her. The steady fall of snow and the cool breeze through the frozen tree limbs muffled the slap of their bodies coming together.

Much later, Lucy lay in his arms, the snow melted away from them, his magic cocooning them with artificial warmth. She'd abandoned all inhibitions, riding him under the moonlight, and making all sorts of wonderful sounds. She was wild and she was his.

He ran his hands along her smooth arms, back and forth. His.

Mine.

She sighed and nuzzled into his neck. "Yes," she said, as if she read his mind.

"Yes," he agreed and pulled her closer. Maybe she could read his mind. He certainly anticipated her needs and wants. Maybe he could read her mind, too. The idea of channelling

Lucy wasn't as scary as it was when he first realized the possibility. He was still himself, but with Lucy, he was more. Better.

If only he could complete the bond. She was here, with him, and yet his skin itched to transform again and search for the missing part of him.

"What's wrong?" Lucy lifted her head from his shoulder.

"Nothing," he assured her.

"Is it the bauble?"

He ran his hand along her back and traced circles without answering. Of course it was the bauble.

"Why don't you just ask her to give it back?"

Damian squeezed her to him. "I don't want to draw attention to myself, or tip off her lawyer. Even if I did ask nicely, Raven's don't part with shiny things voluntarily."

"It's worth a shot."

"Maybe." Or maybe he'd find a way to get close to Arabia and take back what was rightfully his.

He sighed and released his grip on Lucy before he hurt her. He should be ecstatic. Naked, with his claimed mate, yet...yet the absence of his golden mating bead hung in the air like a looming threat, waiting to poison this moment.

CHAPTER NINETEEN

JAILHOUSE BAUBLE

Sunday, December 9th

Damian twisted his charmed ring and merged with the group of loud talking ravenborn gathered at the Stillwater Correctional facility. With Arabia's boy-toy lawyer determined to stake a claim near the exit, his only concern was blending with the raven shifters who'd converged on Stillwater to visit their imprisoned princess.

His glamour darkened his eyes, made his stature appear diminutive and provided a diversion effect. With a magical sleight of hand encompassing his whole body, anyone who looked at him would think he belonged and then the subtle magic would gently guide them to look elsewhere. In a room packed with ravenborn, no one should consider him too closely, and they were too busy discussing some poor sac named "Moon Moon" to pay him any attention.

Damian didn't relax, though. Most raven shifters were capable of manipulating power. Arabia was a strong witch, and she wasn't the only one from her conspiracy. He needed to remain loose and fluid to flow with the noisy congress. The shifters talked, bellowed and barked laughter at one another as if they attended a festive family reunion instead of a prison to visit their incarcerated family member.

The answering energy of his magical bauble called to him somewhere in the room. Hidden beneath a layer of cloaking, now that he actively searched for it, the bead pulsed with energy. As a powerful warlock and griffin, nothing and no one could block him from what was his.

Rip them to shreds, his griffin snarled. *Fuck 'em all up, swoop in and snatch what is ours.*

If only it was that easy. Damian pushed down his griffin.

Hippo squawked.

He needed to remain calm and relaxed or else his glamour would falter and a room full of beady eyes would swivel toward him. He swallowed his anger and meandered through the crowd, brushing past flashy clothes, shiny accessories, and raven scents to slowly make his way toward the call of his bauble.

There! The crowd parted and he glimpsed a clearing. The woman with midnight hair cascading down her back sat on the opposite side of the visitor table clad in a god-awful orange prison jumpsuit. The harsh fluorescent lighting washed her out and left her looking drained. Arabia Jensen.

Somehow, she managed to hide his bauble from the prison guard who processed her and collected all her personal items before admitting her to her cell. Was this a good thing or a bad thing? On one hand, at least he wouldn't have to break into the prison's vault. But on the other hand, gaining access to Arabia in jail would prove more difficult.

Damian glanced back at the lawyer. Chase Baron stalked toward the exit along with a ravenborn man. Both stiff with flat faces. Huh. Maybe after he grabbed his bauble, he'd catch a fight in the parking lot.

"Visitation hours are over," a guard bellowed. "Please exit the center."

Damian groaned. The entire conspiracy converged on Arabia to hug her, whisper words of encouragement and say goodbye.

He maneuvered closer to the exit the guard would have to take. He'd have to catch her before she was removed from the room. But where was the bead? He couldn't exactly search her body while her entire family looked on and the guards stood by. He couldn't glamour into a prison employee without privacy, and he certainly couldn't freeze time. He was powerful, but not *that* powerful.

A guard pulled Arabia from the fray as she waved and blew kisses. Now was his chance. He honed in on his essence. His bauble was definitely on Arabia somewhere. He stepped forward to intercept the guard and prisoner.

"Charming..." A woman stepped into his path.

Damian pulled up short.

"...to meet you," the woman continued, a wide smile.

He stepped to the right. The woman moved in his way again. He stepped to the left. Again, the woman shifted her position like they were doing one of those old antiquated dances where the partners couldn't touch. Maybe he should throw her out of his way?

Damian peered over her shoulder as the guard and Arabia slipped through the prison door. Dammit! He missed his chance.

His magic sizzled down his arms and he turned to the woman who dared to get in his way.

With platinum blonde hair and striking blue eyes, Damian did a double take. She stuck out in a crowd of dark-haired, dark-eyed ravenborn like a porcupine at a nudist colony. How had he not noticed her before?

Her smile widened. "I'm no expert, but I don't think it wise to tackle an inmate in such a crowded room."

What? "Do I know you?"

She leaned in and pressed her fingers to her lips.

"That's not exactly helpful."

She shrugged. "Looked like you had violence on your mind. I thought it best to intervene."

"Not violence, exactly. I'm not a fan of this whole situation." He didn't care about Arabia's fate at this point. He wanted his bauble back.

"Of course not." A small smile tugged at her full lips. She smelled sweet and faintly of fruit. "We're all just pawns to the gods."

His eyebrows rose. "I control my own fate, thank you."

She laughed, the sound of silver bells cascading over the room.

Damian glanced around the room. Nobody else noticed.

"It didn't look like you were in control of anything a few minutes ago," she said.

Well, that was just…accurate. How could he argue against a valid point? He'd been a step or two away from making a huge mistake, the need to get his gold bead from Arabia potent and still coursing through his veins. He *had* to get that bauble. Lucy was vulnerable without it. "Thank you for *stepping* in."

She winked and walked away.

CHAPTER TWENTY

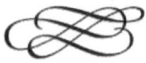

THE SILVERFOX PHENOMENON

Lucy flopped on the couch against the far wall of the café. Today had been long. Maybe Damian was right. She should promote Tanner to manager and hire more full-time staff. They had enough business to support it and she needed a break. If she kept burning the candle at both ends, eventually, she'd run out of wax.

She looked at her kingdom, purchased with every cent to her name and the small savings account her mom left her. With the open sign and lights to the main room switched off, only the light from outside illuminated the area. Moonlight danced along the tabletops and the dark winter night beckoned her to come out and play.

Later, she though. *With Damian.*

Over the years, she lived and breathed all things caffeine, and this little coffee shop thrived. It held her heart...until now.

Now, an overly-proud griffin who misread social cues captivated her.

How the hell had she let that happen? It didn't take away from her love for this place or dedication to her work, but even now, she sensed her priorities shifting. Balancing out.

What if Tanner and the new crew let this place get dirty?

She shivered and clutched her cleaning spray.

You are *ridiculous*, Whispurr said.

Lucy grumbled and hoisted herself off the couch before she sunk into it and never got up again. She needed to finish her closing duties. Then she could relax. Squatting by the pastry display case, she hummed a Christmas tune and worked on removing the oily fingerprints.

The door chimed and a gust of cold air burst into the café.

"You're early," she called over her shoulder. "I'm almost done."

"I think you have more serious concerns at the moment than cleaning." A deep male voice, who was decidedly not Damian, spoke behind her. His menacing scent hit her. Augustus.

She whirled around and pointed the spray bottle at the intruder. Yeah, like that would help.

Augustus laughed.

Dark bands of magic slammed into her, battering the magical griffin shield encasing her. She dropped the bottle.

"Now that I'm expecting it, your lover's magic won't provide as much of a deterrent." Augustus's once handsome face twisted into something more cruel and ugly. His gaze darkened and the magic pulsed.

Slammed against the display case, Lucy pushed against the powerful force. If she could angle her body, she'd slide off the glass and travel over the counter. At least then, she'd have a physical shield against his magic.

"How?"

"How am I out?" Augustus' face screwed up in a cruel grin. "I told that hulking detective of yours I'd be out right away. And I was. What took longer was waiting for him to skedaddle from your side long enough for me to pay you a visit."

"Why?" She gasped against the magic.

Augustus frowned, but the force plastering her against the case didn't ease up. "Why what?"

"Why...target me?"

Augustus tilted his head, a movement so reminiscent of a cat he could pass for one. His magic was all wrong, of course. No way was this guy a big cat shifter. He dabbled with something darker and more sinister. "Why not?"

She should've sprayed him with the cleaner when she had the chance.

"This is revenge, pure and simple. As for why I targeted your business, I should've picked someone else to start with. I see that now." He stepped forward and the magic grew stronger. He rotated his wrists, murmuring an incantation under his breath. As he walked closer, more dark bands streamed from his body and wound around each other to form an object. Was that some sort of arrowhead pointed at her? "You seemed so sweet and vulnerable. Yet, you and your boyfriend managed to ruin all my carefully laid plans."

Throwing bricks through windows was a carefully laid plan? Either this guy had a demented sense of the world or he wasn't as much of an evil mastermind as he thought.

The door chimed again and Damian walked in. He froze, his gaze snapping back and forth. Understanding clicked in and he snarled. Magic erupted from his body and rushed toward Augustus. Like a striking lightning bolt, white-gold energy streaked across the room.

The dark warlock grunted and flung out a hand. More magic, vibrating with a tang of death flew from his hand and crashed against Damian's. Sparks flew. The powers collided and pushed back and forth against each other.

Lucy remained pinned against the display case unable to move or help.

Her mate swore and stepped forward, his magic drove

harder against Augustus', sending it back toward the other warlock. Damian was winning and he hadn't shifted yet.

Augustus' gaze darted back and forth. Fear flashed across his gaze, and then he made eye contact with her. The terror slipped away and cold calculation returned. With a smirk, he glanced at Damian before shoving all his power into the deadly object pointing at her.

"No!" Damian flung his hand out.

Augustus released the arrowhead of death. It flew through the air and across the short distance. Time slowed as Lucy remained helpless, stuck watching her own demise barrel toward her. She squeezed her eyes shut.

The arrowhead struck against her shield. The force of impact rocked her body and slammed her back into the display case. Glass crunched.

And...and she wasn't dead.

She popped open one eye. The arrowhead clattered to the floor and evaporated. Augustus was gone. Damian raced toward her. The evil wind pinning her in place fell away. She slipped from the cracked case into Damian's arms. His eagle and lion scent curled around her, kneading her bruised skin.

"Are you okay?" His hands flew over her body checking for injuries.

She glanced up at her mate. "Why am I not dead?"

Damian's lips flattened into a straight line. "I got an additional shield around you in time to block the death arrow. This wouldn't have happened if you'd had the bauble. You wouldn't have needed an extra shield."

His expression said he contemplated immense violence. She wouldn't want to be the thief or Augustus right now.

"Forget the gold bead. Where did Augustus go?"

"That coward ran off the moment I was distracted."

"I can't believe he escaped again." When her energy returned, the anger would come with it, but right now exhaustion pulled at her limbs. All she wanted to do was curl up in the safe heat of Damian's arms and sleep.

"You know what they say," Damian growled. His body vibrated. His griffin flashed across his gaze. "Three times a charm. If I see that man again, I will kill him."

"Damian, I—"

"And you will not stop me. I mean it." His arms tensed around her.

"I wasn't going to try. I'm sorry I stopped you before."

"Not as sorry as he will be."

She glanced at the café's door. Wherever Augustus went, he was long gone. Again. After tonight, though, Augustus would have Damian's measure. He was prepared to attack Lucy tonight. Next time, he'd be ready for Damian. Who knew what awaited her lover on the other side of that door if he left now, or even left later to find this mysterious businessman.

"Don't leave."

"I just watched an evil warlock fling a death arrow at you. For a second, I thought my shield was too late. I'm not going anywhere."

"You're not battling an intense need to rip off heads?"

Damian smiled, all teeth and sheer malice. If she thought for one second it was aimed at her and not his thoughts, she'd probably pee herself in fear. And she didn't scare easily.

"Oh, I want to rip the limbs off that asshole," Damian growled.

"But?"

"But ensuring you're safe is more important."

"Does Hippo agree?"

Damian's smile turned tender and he nodded. The tension around his mouth and neck relaxed. Finally, her Damian had returned. "Hippo wants to take you home."

Lucy relaxed into his arms and let him hoist her up in one swift movement as if she weighed less than a bag of potatoes.

"I'll hunt tomorrow."

Lucy froze. "Don't go chasing problems, Damian."

"Lucy."

"I'm serious. Augustus is long gone and I don't think he'll return. Did you see his face? You scared him shitless."

Another toothy smile spread across her mate's face. His expression turned thunderous and his eyes flashed eagle gold for a second before returning to normal. "Good."

CHAPTER TWENTY-ONE

GRAND THEFT BAUBLE

Friday, December 21ˢᵗ

Damian lay in bed with Lucy in his arms, her soft skin heating his side. Safe and unharmed. He should be relaxed and enjoying the moment with his mate, but the absence of his bauble itched at his skin. If she'd held his gold bead, she would've had more protection against Augustus.

Though he promised his mate not to chase after the vile man, that didn't stop him from making inquiries and opening an investigation.

Hippo screeched. *You still need to do something.*

What exactly?

Hippo grumbled. *If you have to wait to go after the guy, at least get the bead back.*

Tension knotted his shoulders at the thought of his other pressing problem. Even if he used his considerable power to break into the magically-protected prison or posed as a guard to infiltrate the area holding, he'd still have to accost an adept ravenborn witch in her jail cell and search her for the missing bead. Arabia Jensen would hardly stand still, and if he knocked her unconscious or killed her, he'd have to face the wrath of the gods.

His phone vibrated on the nightstand. He reached across Lucy and his arm grazed her naked breasts.

Mmmm. He knew how he'd rid his mind of the nagging internal griffin who insisted he track his bauble.

He answered the phone. "Charming."

"It's me," Mateo said.

"Any signs of Augustus Reid?"

Lucy stretched out beside him. He watched her limbs straighten and muscles elongate. He ran his hand down the smooth skin of her stomach. She purred.

"No, and the office building was purchased with a shell company. We passed it on to the financial team, but it could take months to track down an authentic identity."

"Fuck."

"Yeah. We might have to give it to a bounty hunter."

His cellphone creaked under his increased grip, the plastic threatening to crack. He'd go after the man himself, but he couldn't leave Lucy. She might be a feisty feline, but she didn't have the protection of the bauble and if Augustus lurked nearby, waiting for an opportunity to pounce—an opportunity like Damian racing off to chase a ghost trail—he wanted to be ready.

Damian eased his grip on the phone. "So the turd vandalized the businesses on Main Street to drop their value and motivate the owners to sell?"

"Apparently."

"And skipped Laura."

"Well, you know Laura."

He did. Laura's Clover Club hadn't been targeted, yet, but her fierce reputation probably deterred Augustus from attacking. Luckily, Augustus didn't know Laura. The cougar shifter wasn't as confident or ferocious as she let on—she had cracks in her armor, just as Lucy wasn't as tame as everyone thought.

Oh, his mate was loving and generous, but her backbone was made of metal alloy. She might be a lynx on the street, but she was a minx in the bed. She'd also be an absolute savage to protect her business and loved ones. Savage. "Want to switch surnames?"

"What?" His partner sounded incredulous. "No."

Lucy giggled. With her shifter abilities, she'd hear both sides of the conversation.

"Never mind," he muttered.

"I'm calling about the other case," Mateo said.

What other case? He was only involved with...Oh. That one. "Arabia Jensen?"

"Yeah. Is it safe to talk?" He meant to ask if it was okay to talk about the case in front of Lucy. He would've heard her giggle. Damn shifters and their heightened senses.

"Yeah. Lucy knows."

"And she still wants to be with you?"

"Shut up."

"Hi, Mateo," Lucy piped up after she finished another stretch.

"Hey, Luce," Mateo said.

"So what's this about Arabia? Isn't her court date today?" Damian asked.

"Yeah. The case was going well. White got away with a half-truth on the stand regarding your identity, and then suddenly the lawyers met with the judge behind closed doors."

Damian sat up. This couldn't be good. "What about?"

"They know," Mateo said. He didn't need to elaborate. There was only one reason his partner would call him with this news.

Damian cursed. "How?"

"Laura. Apparently, Baron paid her to look into the anonymous caller. She found one of your police-issued bugs."

Damian squeezed his eyes closed. He'd meant to go back and retrieve them. He'd forgotten all about the devices once he discovered his bauble missing.

Lucy moved to kneel behind his tense back. Her hands slipped up his shoulders and began kneading.

"An out of town agency secured Arabia's cabin and at least one of them has a loose tongue. There's whisperings around town now about a griffin. I'm not sure who knows what, but it's out there. It won't take long for people to make the connection."

Damian clutched the phone until it squeaked. No. No, he couldn't squish it. All that hard work and now the whole town knew his identity. Oh sure, only a select few for now, but it was just a matter of time. "Dammit!"

"Apparently, you left tracks."

Damian counted down from ten. When that soothed his nerves, he repeated the action. "Do you have any good news?"

"Well, my job is secure."

"That actually is good news." He'd never forgive himself if his actions caused his partner and only friend to lose his job.

"Yours probably isn't, though," Mateo said.

Damian looked at Lucy. "I have all I need here."

"They want to bring you in for questioning," Mateo added.

"I'll come in when I'm good and ready."

If they fired him, they fired him. He didn't need the money. Besides, now that his identity as a griffin was out, or at least soon to be out, he doubted the PD would let him go. They'd find a loophole. Oh, they might slap his wrists or make him take one of those painful courses on police procedure, but he'd keep his job.

"How does this affect the case?" he asked Mateo.

"Apparently, the defense cut a deal. Arabia's set to be released."

"When?" Damian leapt from the bed.

Lucy fell forward, belly-flopping on the mattress after the unexpected move. She had the nicest ass. If he bent down right now, he could rake his teeth along the plump curve. Maybe move in behind her and...

"Now," Mateo said.

His griffin surged, bashing through the constraints Damian used to hold it in check. He managed to squeak out one word. "Thanks."

He hung up and threw the phone on the bed. In minutes, he was dressed and stalking to the door. Lucy stayed out of the way, but trailed him through the house.

He stuffed on his boots and grabbed his keys.

"Damian?" Lucy called out after him.

"Yeah."

"Don't do anything stupid."

"Define stupid." No point in denying the idiocy of some of his recent actions.

"Don't hurt them."

Damian growled. "She stole from me."

"I know, but...you can't put a price on a clear conscience."

Yes, he could. It was the price of his golden bauble. If they refused to hand it over, he wouldn't show mercy.

"Damian..."

"I'll try to be..." He ground his teeth.

"Good?" Lucy suggested.

"Yeah...that."

Taillights slipped over the hill. Got them! Damian accelerated. Tailing someone was a lot more difficult than the movies made it out. Especially at night with headlights.

Luckily, he didn't need to follow them closely and his eagle eyesight helped him navigate the windy roads. There were only a few exits from the town. Chase and Arabia headed south out of the Sierra Nevada Mountains. The winding mountainous road were perfect for his plan.

Damian let the town fall away behind him. Lightning streaked in the exposed sky above the tree tops. Thunder rolled, loud and heavy, jostling the SUV. Normally, Damian's rage impacted the local weather and in the winter could cause thundersnow, but this wasn't him. He wasn't angry. He had a plan and it was time to implement it.

Either someone else created this rare weather phenomenon, or Mother Nature decided to treat Damian to the real thing. Lovely. The storm was almost directly above him now. Griffin energy spiraled up, weaving a complex shield around him and filling the interior of the vehicle.

Enough of this, Hippo growled.

Damian pressed down the accelerator. When Baron's car came back in sight, he flicked on the high beams. Snow bombarded his windshield, making it appear like he traveled through space on a hyperspace jump. His wipers swished back and forth, frantically attempting to clear the fat snowflakes as they caked on the glass.

Come on, asshole. Pull over.

Bright lights illuminated the interior of the luxury sedan ahead of him. Wide eyes flashed in the rear-view mirror. Instead of pulling over, the sedan picked up speed.

Idiot! These roads weren't made for speeding in winter. Damian pressed his foot down and pulled the SUV closer to the car. The engine roared. He honked his horn. "Come on. Pull over."

Damian punched the gas again. The sedan didn't accelerate fast enough. A dull thud of metal joined the rolling thunder. The impact of his SUV's bumper against the other vehicle propelled the sedan forward.

Whoa.

Calm down, his griffin hissed. *We want them alive, not off the road.*

Not helping.

He hadn't meant to give the car a love tap. He only wanted to impress upon them the importance of pulling over.

Damian took a deep breath. Adrenaline punched through his veins. He loosened his tight grip on the steering wheel. Chase wasn't pulling over. Stubborn wolf. Damian needed to calm down. He eased off the gas, and the sedan sped forward, putting distance between them.

Damian looked ahead, through the snow splattering his windshield. His high beams caught the curve in the road. Fuck! He pumped the brakes, willing his heavy vehicle to slow down enough before entering the deadly turn. His magic rushed out, creating a cushion of air resistance. His momentum decreased. The tires slid on the icy road, but the SUV slowed. Damian released a long breath and watched as the sedan flew toward the bend in the road.

Oh no.

With too much speed, the sedan soared around the corner and crashed against the guardrail. Metal shrieked and groaned. The car careened against the flimsy guardrail, rolled and plowed down the mountain slope.

Damian cursed and pulled over to the side of the road at the next straight stretch. He stepped from his SUV. He was always better at flying than driving—an imperfection he loathed to admit and would deny vehemently.

A sonic boom rocked the night. The forest fell silent. Damian jumped. "No!"

Now you've done it, Hippo snarled.

He didn't want either of them dead. Especially not the ravenborn. He wanted them to pay.

Another dark thought streaked through his mind. *The bead.* Dread sliced up his spine like blades made of ice. Was his mating bauble in the car? Surely he would've felt his essence destroyed.

Damian pushed his magic forward and swept the area. Multiple signatures rebounded to him, including human corvid and lupine signatures. And his bead. His essence called to him like a homing beacon. Chase and Arabia lived and they were on the run. Damian let out a long breath.

Though relieved, his blood still boiled, hot and volatile. He didn't want to kill them, but they needed to atone for their actions. No one stole from him. Because of Arabia's theft, his mate had been vulnerable to Augustus' attack. If he'd been a second later, she would've died. Even now, she sat in his warded home without the mating bauble and the extra protections it granted.

Damian slammed closed the door to his SUV and stomped into the forest, making his way down the mountain side. His boots slapped in the slush and mud. The sweet hint of pine, fir and juniper wound around him with each gust of cold air. The forest life remained silent, sensing the predator amongst them, or maybe anticipating the events to come. Wet snow and sleet continued to fall, and in seconds, Damian's clothes were encrusted with ice. He snarled.

After he searched for the signatures again, he estimated at least a quarter of a mile separated him from his targets. Flying through a densely treed forest in griffin form was awkward as fuck and made searching for prey tedious. He could fly above the treeline in the hopes he'd spot them with his enhanced eyesight, but with a natural, unpredictable thundersnow storm raging above them, he'd rather not.

Fuck this. Time to call the hounds. He refused to spend all night trudging through sodden forest to find two thieving lovebirds. Well, one thieving lovebird and her lapdog. He pulled on his magic and reached deep into a forbidden place—a place of darkness and pain. He pushed his power into the call and two hell hounds answered. Should he call more? No. Overkill.

He shifted a finger to a talon and ran the sharp edge along his palm. Blood flowed freely, splattering to the ground with the unrelenting sleet.

With a pact made, the hellhounds' violent energy tethered to him and they materialized a foot away.

Large crinkled snouts gaped open, showing off their curved black tusks perfect for ripping into the soft underbelly of prey. Snow and ice coated the scales covering their keg-shaped bodies. Unlike moose, so ugly they're cute, hellhounds were so ugly they were grotesque. They waited for his command.

Damian wound his magic around each of them, sending a mental image of their target. "Find them. Bring them to me."

Three beady eyes from each hound blinked at him. Hellhounds weren't the brightest beasts, but their simplicity and desire to please their master made them perfect for this task.

"Go," he commanded.

The hound on the right yowled and took off, bounding past Damian. The second echoed the call and gave chase. Damian watched their rows of spines and stubby tails disappear in the stormy night.

The hounds might be ugly as hell, but they were great at chasing. They'd find his targets, flush them out and round them up faster than he could. Scaring the crap out of Chase and Arabia was just an added bonus.

The wind picked up, cold and miserable, and bordering gale force. He should be home with Lucy, basking in the warmth of her body and making her say all sorts of dirty things along with those low mewling sounds.

The calls and squeals of the hounds carried through the

night. What the hell was that? He told them not to hurt them. He specifically told them to bring the criminals to him.

You sure about that? his griffin asked.

Damian paused. *Wait a minute.*

He hadn't specified *how* to return Arabia and Chase to him. Damian groaned. If those dumb mutts ate his bauble...

He stomped past a line of pines and halted. A large raven perched on a nearby branch watching the scene through beady eyes. Arabia. One hound lay dead under a fallen tree and the other fought the wolf. Well, on one hand, he didn't need to worry about the hounds gulping down his mating bead, but on the other hand, this hadn't gone exactly as planned.

Did you really believe you could herd a werewolf anywhere? Hippo said.

Damian scowled. His griffin made an excellent point. He'd never hear the end of this.

As Damian stepped closer, Chase ripped out the throat of the hound. Blood sprayed from the wound and the hound fell to the ground limp. Yup, sending hellhounds to herd an alpha werewolf was definitely a bad idea.

There was no rewind button for life, unfortunately. He may as well go along with the current situation. "Oh, bravo! That was marvelous." Slow clapping, more for himself than Baron, Damian approached the couple. He walked past one of the dead hellhounds. Such a waste. Sure, they were from the abyss and all, but he kind of liked them. At least they'd respawn in the underworld. They weren't really dead so much as sent back home. They wouldn't pay for his mistake.

Chase turned to him, anger flashing in his lupine gaze. The lawyer straightened and shifted partially, presenting a man-wolf hybrid form. Not all werewolves could partially shift. This alpha was strong.

"You think this is funny?" Chase growled.

"Well, no. Not really. On the whole, I'm far from amused."

He raised his hands and pulled on his magic. If Baron attacked him, he'd be ready. The werewolf would find him a far greater challenge than the minions of the Underworld. His power crackled in his veins.

"What the hell is wrong with you?" Chase asked.

"What's wrong with me?" These two killed his dogs and stole his shit and had the nerve to ask what was wrong with *him*? He placed a hand to his chest as if mortally wounded. It was either ridiculing this couple or outright fighting. Lucy would want him to find the peaceful solution, to be a good griffin. Apparently, this was the best he had.

"Yeah, you. Why are you stalking my woman?" Baron demanded.

"Your woman?" He glanced at Arabia. They had zero chemistry together, why would he stalk her?

"You heard me."

Damian wanted nothing to do with Arabia, he just wanted his bauble back. Oh, wait. The fire in his veins tempered a little. He replayed his own actions of the last few weeks. Understanding punched him with a mean uppercut. Yeah, he looked bad, but it wasn't at all what Chase thought. "Chill. I'm not challenging you for your woman."

"You're not?"

"No."

"Why've you gone to all this trouble, then? Stalking her. Ransacking her house. Setting her up?" Chase vibrated, his gaze flashing, his weight shifting forward.

The last thing any of them needed was for the wolf shifter to lose control. Damian sent out his magic, offering mellow, calming energy. As long as he kept his voice low, his posture relaxed, remained calm and Arabia didn't do anything stupid, they'd—

As if hearing her name in his thoughts, Arabia flapped her wings and launched from her perch. In seconds, she shifted to reveal her fully-clothed form.

Oh for fuck's sake.

"Damian, stop," she said. "I won't let you hurt him."

He counted down from three before responding. "Hurt him? Now why would I want to do that?"

"Bastard! You tried to kill us!" She stomped her foot. Was that supposed to be threatening? Intimidating? Chase had his hands full with this one.

His fingers itched to pinch the bridge of his nose.

Just fuck them up. Hippo pushed him. *Take our bead and go home to Luce. Much faster.*

Chase reached forward, clamped a hand on his mate's shoulder and hauled her behind him. In any other situation, Damian would've laughed, or at least commiserated. Not tonight. He was wet and cranky and wanted this over.

"That?" Damian said. "I was just playing. If I wanted you dead, you'd be dead already. All I want—"

Chase growled and stalked forward.

Damian groaned. Alpha werewolves were so tiresome to deal with. He'd rather negotiate with an enraged silverback gorilla. At least those beasts had some common sense, with or without their women present.

Damian held up both his hands. He raised his voice so Chase and Arabia could hear him over the growling. "All I want is the return of what is rightfully mine—my stolen property!"

Chase stopped snarling. "What?"

Damian sighed, his shoulders dropping. Chase had no clue what he was talking about, the look on his face almost comical. Arabia hadn't told Baron about the bauble. He glanced at the angry sky overhead. Maybe one of the gods could help him. These two didn't exactly excel at communicating with each other. "Arabia, tell your lover the truth, why don't you?"

Arabia bit her lip and had the decency to look sheepish.

171

"Now, Chase, I can explain. It's not like he's making it sound."

Damian held back a snort. It was exactly as it sounded and now the little thief tried to put a spin on it.

The man-wolf hybrid turned to Arabia. "Is it true? Did you steal from this man?"

"Yes." She tugged at a thin braid almost invisible in the dense mane of hair. Something gold flashed.

Damian leaned forward and narrowed his eyes.

"But it was just a little bauble," Arabia continued. "I didn't think he'd even notice."

Thief! Hippo hissed.

His griffin energy surged up, as impatient and enraged as he was. "Not notice! No one steals from me without me noticing." His control on his griffin slipped. His power surged forward. Fed up with accusations, done with placating and reasoning, the energy simmering beneath the surface ripped through his body with electrifying ferocity. Lightning flashed and thunder rolled.

His griffin emerged under an ice-cold sheet of sleet.

"Shit," Arabia muttered.

"That about sums in it up," Chase said.

Damian roared into the night. His control over his anger snapped. All this talking and he still didn't have his gold mating bead. His mate sat at home, vulnerable to another attack by Augustus. Enough. Fucking enough.

Arabia and Chase mumbled to each other some more. Too much rage flowed through his veins for him to listen. He let the griffin essence roll through him and spill out to the surrounding area.

When his blood stopped boiling, he reined in the griffin power. Speaking in his animal form wasn't impossible for him as it was for others, but awkward. He had to focus on forming the sounds with his beak like a fucking parrot. If he had a choice, he wouldn't speak in this form at all. "I want what's rightfully mine."

"Stay away from my mate," Chase bellowed. "I don't care what she stole. You're not coming near her."

Damian didn't give a shit what Chase cared about any more. He circled the wolf shifter and assessed Chase's gait, the speed of his reactions and the power of his limbs.

Arabia screeched like some wanton banshee and tripped. Her arms flailed, trying to take flight in human form and she fell face first in the mud.

Her hair whipped forward, and a flash of gold caught his eye. His bauble! Woven into the black strands of Arabia's braid, his mating bead stood out in the dark.

Mine!

Damian lunged forward. Chase snarled and attacked, barrelling into Damian before he could claim his property.

Damian reared up and absorbed most of the impact, digging in his talons as they locked onto one another. Lightning flashed in the background. A boom of thunder rocked the night. The ground under Damian's hind legs shook.

Without warning, the slope disappeared. Like the coyote after a botched roadrunner attack, they hovered, briefly suspended in air while they remained entangled before they plummeted down the hill. The impact knocked the air from his lungs. A dark mushy wave of sodden earth rolled them downward. The force of the tumbling ripped Chase from Damian's grip. The dirt bowled Damian over, again and again, until up and down were two abstract thoughts. A bone snapped. Pain streaked down his wing. Mud slathered his body and slammed down his mouth. He shut his eyes and waited for the spinning to stop.

The landslide of sludge slowed, easing Damian to a halt as the ground leveled out.

Shit. That hurt. Mud in his eyes, mud in his beak, mud in his nostrils. Pain radiated down one of his wings. Squashed by a pile of soggy dirt, Damian squealed.

Light footsteps approached, slapping against the mud. Arabia turned to him, dark gaze flashing. "Damian, you're a cop! You're supposed to be better than this. If the bauble I stole from you is so damn important, why didn't you just ask for it back?"

Well, that just sounded too fucking reasonable. Annoyance slashed through his bruised body. No way in hell would Arabia return the priceless bauble to him with a simple request.

Didn't Lucy suggest something similar? Hippo asked.

"It's mine. You shouldn't have taken it in the first place," he said. Wow. That didn't sound petulant. Not at all.

"I may have some kleptomania tendencies I need to work on."

Damian groaned. That's it? That was the grand apology for stealing from him?

Arabia grabbed her braid and yanked on the bead. "In my defense, I'm not always even aware when I take things."

"I'm not your therapist. I just want it back." He pulled free from the sludge and stood. Globs of mud fell off and splattered the ground. Dirt still clung to his feathers and fur. One of his wings bent at the wrong angle. The shooting pain had been replaced with an impressive throb.

"Hold your horses...I'm working on it."

"My patience is wearing thin..." He held his breath and pushed his broken wing out. The movement and his magic forced the bone to snap back into place. Some of the pain eased away. His magic continued to weave around his wing, knitting together the broken bone and accelerating his healing. In a few minutes, he'd recover enough to fly.

"Arabia," Chase said. "I'm adding this to my list of things I never thought I'd hear myself say. Give the nice griffin back his bauble."

"Got it! Here." Instead of walking over to gently hand him

his treasured item, the little brat threw the bead at him.

Damian snarled and snatched the bead from the air with his talons. "Thank you. I'd say it's been a pleasure, but that would be a lie."

Crouching low, he gathered strength and pushed off the ground. He beat his wings. His mending one complained, shooting pain down the metacarpus, but held in the strong storm winds. He only needed to make it to the car. Tonight, he'd sleep beside his mate and bask in her heat.

Damian pushed open the door to his home and stepped out of the miserable night. Lucy's scent greeted him and sent tingles through his cold limbs. His boots splashed mud onto the door mat and melting snow dripped off him as if he stepped from a dirty ice bath without toweling off. The short drive home had done little to better the situation.

"Hey, honey," he called out. "I'm home."

Lucy chuckled from the living room. "That sounds so wrong."

"But you kind of like it."

"I kind of do." Lucy turned the corner to the mudroom and stopped short. "What did you do?"

His eyes widened with his best attempt at innocence. He encompassed a lot of things, but nothing close to that concept. "I got the bauble back."

Instead of elation, she scowled and folded her arms over her chest. She'd dressed since he left and if the smooth scent of coffee was any indication, she'd heavily caffeinated to stay up and wait for his safe return. "Damian."

He peeled off his jacket and hung the bedraggled garment on a hook. His hand throbbed from the healing break. Mud and water dripped onto the tile floor of the mudroom and splattered against the baseboards. "There might've been a flipped car. But that wasn't my fault. The idiot was driving too—"

"Damian."

"And hellhounds." He winced. "I summoned hellhounds."

"Damian!"

"She *stole* from me."

"Are they alive?"

Damian's head snapped back. "Of course, they're alive. I'm not a monster."

She unfolded her arms to jab an accusatory finger at him. "And you needed to find out where the bauble was first."

Damian looked away.

Hah! Nailed it, Hippo barked with laughter.

Silence stretched and weighed on his shoulders.

Damian cleared his throat and held the golden bead out. Dirty water dripped down his fingers and onto its smooth surface before falling to the ground. "Still want me?"

Three simple words spoken plainly. Yet, his entire happiness rested on her response. Maybe he should've dried his hands and cleaned the bauble first. Maybe he should go down on one knee and propose. Maybe he should—

"Absolutely."

A large, genuine smile broke across his face. He couldn't stop it if he tried.

"But we need to teach you some manners. Some social etiquette."

He nodded. "And morals."

"Those too."

"Learn to be a good griffin."

"Exactly."

He stood and swooped her up in his arms in a single motion. "And I know just where we should start."

Lucy laughed and he carried her to the bedroom.

EPILOGUE

THE WEDDING GIFT

L ucy stood at the kitchen counter with her back to him, tense and focused on something sitting on the granite surface. Her hair shone under the sunlight streaming through the windows. "How was your visit with Mateo and Kiera?"

"Great. I'm glad they worked things out." Those two were so happy it was almost nauseating. Almost. He couldn't begrudge his partner for his relationship when Damian was probably just as sickening with his own happiness. "How was work?"

"Long. I missed you." She didn't turn to greet him, which was odd, and kept her attention on whatever sat on the counter.

He walked over and slipped his arms around her, pulling her into him, her shirt soft under his hands. Not as soft as her skin. She fit him perfectly. The tension left her body. He rested his head on top of hers and peered down at the mystery item. A gift wrapped in pretty pink paper with white polka dots and a yellow bow sat inconspicuously in front of them.

"What's that?" he asked.

"A wedding gift."

"A little late, isn't it?" Damian squashed the urge to preen. He squeezed Lucy and admired her wedding ring. The gold bauble sat as the center stone instead of a diamond. His essence in the bead and the charm he'd cast around the ring coated Lucy with protection and marked her as his. It also melded their lives together. Now they had plenty of lifetimes to enjoy their bonding.

"It's from Arabia."

Damian tensed.

"Think it's safe to open?"

"Probably not."

"We can't just chuck it." Lucy leaned forward and sniffed again. "Smells fruity."

"I'm fresh out of Hazmat suits, you?"

She shook her head. "What about opening it in the vault?"

"We'd still be inside with it, unless you've hoarded military grade robots I don't know about?" Images of his horde flooded his mind. The vault would put the local banks to shame. Cloaked with heavy magic, the impenetrable structure hidden in their basement housed all sorts of priceless gems, statues and other items, none of which were robots capable of helping them out with Arabia's gift.

"If anyone has a hording issue in this relationship, it's you," Lucy said.

"Damn straight." He kissed her neck and inhaled her wild scent. His magic sparked against the box and streaked inside. The probe came back empty. "There's no malicious magic inside, and I doubt the raven princess would stoop to something as mundane as a bomb."

"I say we just open it." Without waiting for a response, Lucy reached forward and pulled the end of the bow. The ribbon fell away and his mate attacked the wrapping paper. Cats and paper. Honestly. Mateo was the same. Maybe he should invest in one of those laser pointers.

With the dainty wrapping paper in shreds, a decorated gift box made of thick cardboard sat on the kitchen counter. Damian released Lucy so he could stand beside her.

She looked up and winked. She broke the seal and opened the lid. The potent smell of apples and bananas exploded from the box along with the words, *"Pray, hear my words, Arianrhod, one face of the Mother Goddess, Goddess of fertility and fruition. Please accept my humble offering. In return, bless this mated pair, the good griffin and lovely lynx, and deliver unto them the blessed fruit from their union, all be well, so mote it be."*

The spell coiled around Lucy, wrapping around her waist like a protective shield before it soaked in. Lucy stood still for a brief second before she patted her stomach frantically.

The purpose of the spell hit him squarely in the face. Laughter bubbled up his chest and sent him doubling over in a fit.

She turned her wide eyes to him. "What the hell was that?"

Damian waited until the laughter released his chest and he could speak. "A fertility spell."

Lucy's jaw dropped open.

"I hope you're ready for the pitter-patter of little paws."

THE END

Did you enjoy this story? Please leave a review!

Also, check out the other stories in the Old Black Magic World and the Heart's Desire Series. Though they're all standalone stories, they are interconnected with the town, locations and characters.

Watch for other *That Old Black Magic* titles:

Love is the Law by Melissa Snark
Truth or Dragon by Julia Lake Mills
Branded by Ann Gimpel
Beary Sassy by Vonnie Davis
Enchanted by Monica La Porta

ACKNOWLEDGMENTS

A giant thank you to Melissa Snark for inviting me to write in her *That Old Black Magic World*, and for sharing her dashing villain, Damian, with me. Not only did she come up with "Hex Appeal" and "Grand Theft Bauble", the scene in the chapter called *Grand Theft Bauble* contains dialogue from her story. These words are of her creation, not mine, and I wouldn't dream of taking credit for them. The sequence of events in this same chapter was also of her creation, though the words describing them in this book are my own.

The dialogue between Mateo and Damian in the chapter called *The Hasty Retreat*, was created in collaboration with Vonnie Davis.

Thank you to my beta readers: Charlotte Copper, Karilyn Bentley, Maureen Bonatch and Nicole Flockton.

I'd like to thank Monica La Porta for the striking and powerful cover (wowza!) and Lara Parker for editing this creation and all my others. I'm sorry for all the Canadian spellings you had to strike out. Those pesky "U"s just sneak in there.

Thank you to my family and friends for their love, guidance and support, but most of all, thank you to YOU, my fabulous readers, for picking up my creation and following me on this journey. If I'm a new-to-you author, please consider checking out my other books. Happy reading.

ABOUT THE AUTHOR

J. C. McKenzie is a book-loving, gumboot-wearing, unapologetic science geek. She's from an island in the middle of a temperate rainforest, and loves the ocean. J.C. writes predominantly urban fantasy and paranormal romance with sassy heroines and brutish alpha-type men.

Discover more of her books at:
www.jcmckenzie.ca

OTHER BOOKS BY J. C. MCKENZIE

Carus Series:
Shift Happens (Book 1)
Beast Coast (Book 2)
Carpe Demon (Book 3)
Shift Work (Book 4)
Beast of All (Book 5)

Obsidian Flame Series:
Dangerous Dreams (Book 1)
Dangerous Liaisons (Book 2)

That Old Black Magic Shared World:
The Good Griffin (standalone)

Lobster Cove Shared World:
The Shucker's Booktique (standalone)

The Candy Hearts Shared World:
Be My Love (standalone)

KEEP READING FOR A PREVIEW OF

DANGEROUS DREAMS

(AN OBSIDIAN FLAME STORY, BOOK 1)

CHAPTER ONE

THE JOB

The rigid chair grew warm under Lara's leather-clad thighs. Her muscles twitched and begged to run from the opulent waiting room. The glorious taste of coffee coating her mouth earlier had long since turned sour. Waiting had never been one of her strong points.

Sweat pebbled on her nose. She clutched the sheath of her katana sword where it lay across her lap. The nearby clicking of the secretary's fingers on a keyboard and the muted conversations of workers down the hall prevented true silence in the large space.

The impressive office of the Astarot, leader of the entire dragon enclave, towered over the bustling downtown area of Victor. On the top floor, the building swayed in the strong winds constantly plaguing the area. Or maybe the room swayed because of her nerves.

"Mr. Dragoi will see you now." The secretary, with legs

worthy of a runway model and a face to match, nodded her impeccably painted features and tight hairdo toward the double doors on the right.

Lara gulped and stood. Her leather pants creaked. She tugged the knife strapped to her thigh and adjusted her gun belt. With her sheathed sword clutched in one hand, she walked toward the Astarot's office.

Mmmm, Lara's dragon perked up. *Huge building, large waiting room... I wonder what else is—*

Lara shoved her dragon deep into her core and slammed the door on her evil half's wicked thoughts. She slung her sword onto her back and clasped the straps.

No way would she let the Astarot know she was a dragon shifter like him. No way, no how.

Dragon males were all the same. Bull-headed alphas thinking they knew best because of the dangling organ between their legs. Given their notorious superiority complexes and the lack of female dragons, the shifter scene resembled a shitstorm of testosterone fighting for the same prize. No subtlety.

Nope. No interest in having a panting, horny alpha wanting her only for her dragon.

When Lara's supervisor, Herb, called and informed her of today's appointment, she'd balked—the way a rabbit balked when shoved into a den of wolves.

Did the Astarot know?

She'd been so careful. She hadn't shifted in almost half a year and always travelled north to a secluded area for the transformation. No one knew her as a dragon shifter, yet the Astarot had requested her by name. Said he wanted the best, and apparently Herb couldn't convince him "the best" was someone else. For once, Lara appreciated Herb's constant undervaluing of her skills.

The large double doors loomed in front of her. Instead of grabbing the intricately designed dragon handles, she wrapped her knuckles against the smooth wood and took a deep breath.

"Enter."

With her heart in her throat, Lara ran her hands along the smooth handles and pushed open the heavy door. She'd never met Rafael Dragoi, and had hoped to keep it that way. As the leader of not only the Obsidian Dragon Clan, but the whole enclave, he would be a fierce alpha—exhibiting the very best and worst traits of a shifter.

Why had Rafael Dragoi requested her for a job? As far as anyone in her agency was concerned, she was a lowly mage.

I can think of some jobs to do for him, purred her dragon.

A tall man, with broad shoulders and powerful stature, faced the floor-to-ceiling windows with his hands clasped behind his back, presumably watching the world outside.

"Astarot Dragoi," Lara said formally.

The Astarot turned slowly. His power radiated out from him and licked her skin. Flowing over her body, his energy called to her own and sent heat racing through her veins.

Lara stiffened.

Her dragon pressed against the locked cage and moaned.

Wanton harlot.

"Miss Stone." Midnight hair framed chiseled features. His striking dragon-green gaze smoldered as his power rolled over her in sensuous waves.

"A bit tacky to feel up the help, don't you think?" With a mental flick of her hand, Lara slapped his magic away. As a female dragon shifter, she possessed a significant amount of power herself.

Luckily, magic was magic. All energy held its own taste, but the personality of the wielder determined the flavor, not his or her nature. All sorts of powerful entities inhabited the Victor area, existing somewhat peacefully among mundane humans. She posed as a simple mage and as long as Lara kept her dragon suppressed, no one—not even the big, bad Astarot—would deduce the true origin of her magic. As long as no one penetrated her defenses.

Mmm. Let that man penetrate us.

Lara muzzled the horny beast inside her. Yup. Definitely too long since she let her dragon out. Increased libido was one of the side effects of a caged dragon. Between that and her dragon's random and inappropriate comments, Lara might go a bit crazy if she didn't get out of town soon to shift.

Her dragon grumbled and curled up, sulking.

"My apologies." Rafael Dragoi's deep rumbling voice interrupted Lara's thoughts. The Astarot smirked. The resulting dimple showed he hadn't died a slow death from regret for magically groping her. If Lara didn't know better, she'd swear his crinkled eyes indicated he heard the entire exchange with her dragon.

She froze.

Had he? No way. No one had ever made it past her guard. She quickly checked her mental shield. It vibrated with hazy red vitality. Completely intact. No holes. No *penetration.*

Her dragon whined again.

Rafael waved an arm toward a chair. "Please, have a seat."

Sweat plastered the leather pants to her skin. Unease scurried along her spine like starving rodents. Sitting held no appeal. At all. "I'll stand."

He shrugged. "Suit yourself."

Lara's muscles tensed under the scorching scrutiny of the Astarot. When did he plan to enlighten her on the assignment? The silence itched at her skin.

"You requested me by name?" she prodded.

"Yes."

She waited.

He continued to study her.

"Why?"

A slow, knowing smile spread across his face. Lara normally

wanted to swipe such a smug look off a man, but dammit if he didn't make it sexy. The air around them grew thick and heavy. Her dragon hummed and a different kind of heat spread through her body.

Rafael's magic reached out again, like sweet sugared tendrils beckoning her energy to come and play.

"You're the best," he said.

Huh?

Rafael tilted his head. "I requested the best."

"Try again." Lara snorted and cocked a hip. Inside, her nerves quailed. Had he heard her thoughts?

His perfect white teeth flashed. "You're the best who'll look good in a skirt."

Lara's forehead tightened as her brows pinched in. Her cheeks warmed. She clenched her hands into fists. What the hell did that mean?

Rafael chuckled.

Oh crap! She'd definitely said that out loud.

"It means I don't need you to guard an employee or an artifact."

Her heart hammered against her breastbone, premonition casting an icy sheet over her nerves. Surely not. He couldn't mean...

The Astarot's sexy smile disappeared. "I need you to guard me."

READ MORE IN

DANGEROUS DREAMS

AVAILABLE TODAY

www.ingramcontent.com/pod-product-compliance
Lightning Source LLC
Chambersburg PA
CBHW032001170626
46807CB00006B/2591